Rodeo Horse

5

MUSTANG MOUNTAIN

Rodeo Horse

Sharon Siamon

whitecap

Edited by Lori Burwash
Proofread by Elizabeth McLean
Cover photos by Michael E. Burch (mountains) and
    © 2003 Robin Duncan (horse)
Cover design by Roberta Batchelor
Interior design by Margaret Lee / Bamboo & Silk Design Inc.

Printed and bound in Canada.

National Library of Canada Cataloguing in Publication Data

Siamon, Sharon
    Rodeo horse / Sharon Siamon.

    (Mustang Mountain ; 5)
    ISBN 1-55285-467-1

    I. Title. II. Series: Siamon, Sharon. Mustang Mountain ; 5.
PS8587.I225R62 2003   jC813'.54   C2003-911063-X

The publisher acknowledges the support of the Canada Council and the
Cultural Services Branch of the Government of British Columbia in making
this publication possible. We acknowledge the financial support of the
Government of Canada through the Book Publishing Industry Development
Program for our publishing activities.

Please note: Some places mentioned in this book are fictitious while others are not.

To Kyleise Linda Kathleen

CONTENTS

ACKNOWLEDGMENTS

I'd like to thank the following people for their help in the research and writing of *Rodeo Horse:*

Lori Burwash, for her excellent and insightful edit;

Lisa Scarlett, Darci and Chelsea L'Hirondelle, who provided inspiration and contributed their knowledge and enthusiasm for barrel racing;

Robin Burwash, manager, Calgary Stampede/Rodeo Ranch for sharing his expert knowledge of rodeo;

Dr. Wayne Burwash, an equine practitioner near Calgary, for his advice on horses and their injuries.

CHAPTER 1

FLYING CHANGE

Sara Kelly prepared for the run of her life. Sara was eighteen, a champion barrel racer. Her horse Sunny loved to run, and he was ready to give her the best he had. Her heart beat wildly, waiting for their turn to race—through the alley toward the first barrel.

It was December, at the Horner Creek Rodeo near Calgary. Sara centered herself in the saddle, imagining a line running from the top of her head through her abdomen to her legs. A thousand-dollar scholarship if they won. Money for her first year of veterinary school, money she needed now that things were so bad on the ranch. Don't think about the ranch now! Sara told herself fiercely. Think about winning! Think about sending Sunny around those barrels perfectly and blazing for the finish line.

Ready! The pounding of Sara's heart became the pounding of Sunny's hooves toward the first barrel. When they crossed the electric eye beam, the clock started running. Right turn around the first barrel, with Sunny in perfect position, his hind end powering him through the turn, then a flying lead change to the next barrel, around to the left. Once more a perfect turn, with Sara looking ahead to the final barrel at the top of the ring.

The next moment, Sara found herself flying through the air as Sunny stumbled coming out of the turn and pitched her over his head. She had no chance to regain her balance. She landed with her left leg twisted beneath her and felt something in her knee snap—then excruciating pain.

She could hear shouting as people raced toward her. She felt Sunny's muzzle in her face, smelled his warm horsey fragrance, but her eyes were squeezed shut with the effort of trying not to scream.

Sara knew what had happened to her. A ligament in her knee, badly torn in a skiing accident when she was twelve, had torn again.

But what had happened to Sunny? That was much more worrying. She would mend, despite the disgusting pain, but a horse with a badly broken leg ... she tried to open her eyes to see him, but the pain was too great.

"Sara! Where are you hurt?" It was Lisa Rogers, her friend and one of the people in charge of this rodeo. "Can you hear me?"

Sara nodded and gripped her knee. "How's Sunny?" she asked through clenched teeth.

"He looks okay."

"Not limping?"

"Not that I can see. C'mon, how about you? Look at me, Sara."

"I … can't, right now." Sara fought off the waves of pain that made her stomach heave. Any slight movement made her want to howl. Now that she knew Sunny wasn't badly injured, there was no keeping that pain away.

"Stay still. The stretcher's coming. Hang on, kid. We'll have you out of here in no time. Hey! you should see how cute the ambulance guys are."

Sara felt Lisa's hand on her shoulder and struggled to swallow the lump in her throat. She knew what this meant. A whole season of barrel racing down the drain. Weeks in a brace, maybe surgery. Her dream of racing at the Calgary Stampede gone. And that meant no cash for school next fall.

"It's okay, Sunny," she whispered when he nickered unhappily near her ear. "I know it wasn't your fault." But what had gone wrong? she wondered. Sunny was usually so sure on his feet. What had brought her flying champion to such a sudden halt?

The ambulance attendants lifted Sara on the stretcher and carried her out of the ring. With her eyes closed and teeth gritted, she could hear the claps and cheers from the Horner Creek crowd.

CHAPTER 2

MOVING WEST

While Sara sped to the hospital, three girls were grooming horses in a big barn on the other side of the continent.

"Horner Creek! We're moving to some place in the middle of nowhere called Horner Creek," Alison Chant announced to her cousin, Becky. She tipped up her chin to keep the tears from rolling down her pale cheeks. "My parents are separating and it's my fault." She grabbed a curry comb and attacked the tangles in her mare's mane.

Becky Sandersen reached out, whether it was to comfort Alison or save the poor mare from the sudden violence of Alison's grooming, she wasn't sure. The little mustang mare had been at Blue Barn Stables for only ten days—she was just getting used to regular grooming and spending time in the crossties. "Take it easy," Becky

warned. "Don't forget that Shadow is still half wild."
She'd been expecting Alison to explode—ever since a
private talk with her parents that morning, Alison had
been acting like a bucking horse in a rodeo chute.

"Poor Shadow," their friend Meg O'Donnell murmured
from the next set of crossties. "She'll think you're mad at
her." All along the row of stalls, aristocratic noses poked out
to see what the fuss was about. Blue Barn was usually a
peaceful place where well-bred horses led pampered lives.

"Can you blame me?" Alison whirled to face Meg and
Becky. "If she and Patch hadn't come, my parents wouldn't
be splitting."

Meg stroked Patch, her own newly arrived mustang.
Like Shadow, she had lovely cream and brown patches.
One of her eyes was blue, the other brown. The two
paints had traveled together from Wyoming to this riding
stable in New York to start a new life. Meg knew they
would be picking up Alison's unhappy vibrations. Horses
were very sensitive to people's moods.

Meg was tall and leggy, like a young horse herself.
Her blue eyes were wide with sympathy, her ears alert to
the emotion in Alison's voice. Alison was often overdra-
matic and full of her own importance, but this time, Meg
thought, her friend sounded really unhappy. "Maybe
things aren't as bad as you think," Meg told her. "Maybe
you're exaggerating."

"She's not exaggerating." Becky tucked her blonde hair
behind her ears like she always did whenever there was a
crisis. She'd heard the furious arguments at Alison's

house. "But this isn't Shadow's fault, Alison," she protested. "Or yours. Why are you blaming yourself?"

Becky was a complete contrast to her sophisticated city cousin. Brought up in Alberta's ranch country, she had been living with Alison and her parents so that she could go to school with Alison and Meg. Her home, Mustang Mountain Ranch, was isolated and lonely in winter.

"I started the whole break-up," Alison moaned. "If I hadn't made Cousin Terri-Lyn adopt the mustangs and truck them here, none of this would have happened." She tugged on Shadow's tangled mane again. "I'm telling you, when Terri-Lyn rolled up to our house with her beat-up old truck and two horses, my grandmother had a fit. She hates Cousin Terri-Lyn."

"I might have known your grandmother was mixed up in this," Becky muttered. As far as she was concerned, Alison's Grandmother Chant was a tyrant. She'd been dead set against Alison adopting wild horses in Wyoming, against anything connected with Alison's mother's western roots. As far as Grandmother Chant was concerned, her precious son Roger had married beneath him, and she'd tried to cut Alison's mother, Marion, off from the Chant family for years.

"But why would Terri-Lyn cause a fight between your mom and dad?" Meg looked puzzled. "Your mom's on your grandmother's side about her, isn't she?"

"She was, but not anymore." Alison's dark brown eyes were stormy, remembering. "I told Mom I loved Cousin Terri-Lyn and I wouldn't promise not to see her or write to her again. You should have seen my grandmother. I thought her veins would pop." Alison paused.

"Then what?" Meg asked. "I still don't understand."

Brushing away a stray tear, Alison went on. "Then my dad took Grandmother's side and said some really nasty things about your family." She glanced at Becky. "And Mom just ... snapped! I've never seen her so mad. She finally told my dad he had to choose between her and his mother."

"Good for your mother!" Meg cheered.

"Fine for you to say, but he chose Grandmother Chant! My life is shattered." Alison turned back to Shadow and gave a furious tug at her mane. The little paint whinnied in alarm and stepped sideways.

Becky was afraid the mustang would blow up right there in the stall. "Steady, girl," she soothed. "I'm sorry, Alison."

Alison gave an elegant shrug that reminded Becky of old Mrs. Chant, with her straight back and way of looking down her nose at the world. "I wouldn't mind so much, but Horner Creek's a nowhere place near Calgary," she sniffed.

"And what's wrong with Calgary?" Becky's cheeks flared red. Her home was northwest of Calgary.

"It's in Canada." Alison raised her eyebrows. "It's *north* of North Dakota!"

"Could you stay with your dad?" Meg asked hesitantly. She knew Alison's relationship with her father was never easy.

"Oh sure, I *could* live with Dad." Alison rolled her eyes. "But if I did, he and my grandmother would make me give up Shadow and Cousin Terri-Lyn and Aunt Laurie and you ..." She pointed at Becky. "You're part of Mom's family, too."

Becky nodded. Her mother, Laurie, and Alison's mother, Marion, were sisters. "But you wouldn't want to stay with Uncle Roger anyway, would you?" she asked.

Alison went back to grooming Shadow, more gently this time. Lost in thought, she pulled the comb slowly through the mare's long mane. "I hate to move. All my friends are here, and my school. Why should *my* life be wrecked just because my parents can't get along?"

Becky didn't answer. Privately she was excited about this move. There was no school near Mustang Mountain Ranch—it was high in the wilderness, cut off during the winter—so she couldn't live there. But if she moved to Horner Creek with Alison and her mom, she would be closer to home. And she wouldn't miss the Chants! The old woman was a bully, and Uncle Roger a coward.

But Meg was miserable. It was Alison who had welcomed her into the world of horses, taken her on summer trips to Mustang Mountain and, most importantly, given her Patch, her own horse, at last. The horses had been adopted as a pair. If Alison and Becky moved away, her life would come undone.

The big blue barn was silent for a moment as they all took in Alison's news.

Finally, Meg put a comforting arm around her friend's slim shoulders. "Maybe your parents will work things out. Let's hope for the best."

But three weeks later, in the middle of January, Alison, Becky and Meg were saying good-bye. They had loaded Shadow into the horse trailer. Everyone's belongings were already on their way west in a moving van.

"Let's go!" Marion Chant was in the driver's seat. "It took so long to load Shadow, we'll never make it as far as Chicago today." Alison's mother had the same straight nose and determined chin as Alison.

"It's not my fault," Alison snapped. "Shadow doesn't want to go. I don't either. You're going to be sorry you're shipping us out west!"

Becky glanced at her aunt. *My* mom would explode if I talked to her like that, Becky thought. Aunt Marion just gets deadly quiet and sucks in her lips when she's mad.

A cold drizzle had started. It was time to go.

"Bye, Meggie." Becky hugged her friend. "We'll e-mail you from Horner Creek."

Two weeks later, Meg got an e-mail from Alison.

I miss you, Meg. Mom's never home—it seems like her job as a marketing manager is 24/7. And it's horrible at Horner Creek High—worse than I thought. The kids are such hicks, you wouldn't believe. Nobody's heard of the Hamptons or Prada, or even Bloomingdale's. I'm going to die out here. It is so cold.

your frozen friend,
Alison

Meg answered:

I'm sorry you're having such a rotten time. It must be so different for you out there, and it always takes time to get used to a new place. Don't give up! Your mom's job will probably settle down after she's been there awhile and you'll make new friends. Give my love to Shadow, and tell her that Patch misses her.

be happy!
love, Meg

The next message, only a bit more cheerful, was from Becky.

Meggie! How are you and how's Patch? I'm okay. I like the new school, but Alison is being such a snob! She keeps throwing names around and trying to impress people. Which she doesn't. They just think she's weird. Plus, I think we might have a serious problem with Shadow. She's twitchy after the long trip. And we've got her boarded at this rundown little stable. She has no company there, and I know she misses Patch. Alison is so wrapped up in her own problems she has no time for her. Any advice? I miss you.

love, love, love,
Becky

Meg replied:

I miss you, too, and Patch keeps looking for Shadow. I don't know what to say about Alison. She sounded really unhappy in her e-mail. You've got to get her to find Shadow a better barn. Maybe your mom and dad know of some boarding stables around Calgary. Let me know what happens.

Becky answered:

Good idea. The radio-phone at Mustang Mountain isn't working right now, but I'll keep trying my parents. Gotta go. Aunt M needs the computer.

love for now,
Becky

CHAPTER 3

Twin Rocks Ranch

Becky found Shadow's new barn by accident.

On the way home from school, her bus passed a fenced pasture, a lane with a swinging sign and a cluster of trees around a house set back from the road.

"That must be an old ranch," Becky sighed. "I bet it was beautiful, looking out at the Rockies. Now it's just all houses." The suburbs of Calgary were exploding. New towns like Horner Creek sprang up on the snow-covered foothills west of the city like a crusty rash.

"It's depressing," Alison grumbled. "Why do they have to build so many ugly stucco houses?"

"We live in one of them, remember?"

"How could I forget? I wish your dad had never heard about that job for Mom!"

Becky felt a familiar stab of annoyance. She knew Alison blamed her family for the move to Horner Creek. It was Becky's dad, Dan, who had heard about the sales job at the skiwear company, and her mom, Laurie, who'd urged her sister to move west.

"If my mom thought we'd be close to Aunt Laurie and Uncle Dan, she was wrong," Alison went on bitterly. "It's ridiculous. We can't see them because Mustang Mountain Ranch is snowed in, and half the time their radio-phone doesn't even work!"

Becky took a deep breath, smothering the urge to strangle her cousin. "It doesn't help to complain all the time," she muttered.

"It helps *me!*" Alison's forehead scrunched into a knot of angry lines. "Otherwise I'd go crazy. I *am* going crazy. I hate it here. I hate that loser school and all the kids. I hate all this white snow and that big dumb blue sky. Don't you have any clouds out west?"

Becky swung to her feet and gathered her backpack with an angry swoop.

"What are you doing?"

"I'm getting off." Becky grabbed a pole as the bus lurched to a stop. "I'll walk the rest of the way home." She stepped off, turned and caught a glimpse of Alison's startled face peering at her through the mist on the bus window. For a moment she felt guilty about the lost look on her cousin's face, but then shrugged into her backpack. There was only so much of Alison Chant a person could take.

Becky wished Meg were here. Meg always managed to soothe the savage feelings her cousin brought up in her, say something to make them both laugh. But Meg was far away in a suburb of New York City, which now seemed like the far side of the moon.

Without Meg, it was just her and Alison. She could hear her Aunt Marion's voice in her head, saying in her high-pitched voice, "Isn't it lucky you and Alison have each other? You're more like sisters than cousins."

Sisters, ha! That was a good one, Becky thought. Most of the time, she wanted to murder Alison. On good days, they barely got along.

They were as different as their mothers. Marion and Laurie had grown up on a farm in Wyoming. But Becky's mom married a rancher in Alberta, and Alison's mom married a stockbroker in New York. They hadn't been close for years.

So why, when Aunt Marion and Uncle Roger split up, did she suddenly feel a need to be close to her sister? Becky wondered. It didn't make sense, and it was just as crazy to think that she and Alison had anything in common.

As the bus pulled away, Alison watched Becky out the window. Fear and anger churned inside her. How could Becky leave me like this? Where does she think she's going?

Alison turned from the window to see the kids on the

bus staring at her with that mixture of curiosity and dislike she'd seen too often. Then, slowly, they all turned away, as if she didn't exist. She ignored them back, keeping her chin in the air and her eyes fixed forward as the bus swung down the hill.

At first, the kids had laughed at Alison's clothes and her New York accent. Now they ignored her as if she had a contagious disease. I hate them all, Alison thought fiercely. They don't know anything!

✳

Instead of walking toward their housing development, Becky walked back the way the bus had come, her feet crunching on the cold white snow at the edge of the road. She walked as far as the swinging sign and stopped to read it.

"Twin Rocks Ranch," the sign said. "Quarter Horses." The lettering had been proud and fine at one time. Underneath, "Horses for Sale—Riding Lessons and Boarding" had been added by hand.

"Well, I don't need a horse or riding lessons, that's for sure," Becky said out loud. She'd been riding since she was two—there was a picture of her as a baby, sitting proudly on a horse. But at four she'd been bucked off a horse and badly hurt. Becky had never forgotten the fall. The memory of powerful sharp hooves flashing just above her head haunted her.

Since then, Becky had never really trusted horses. You never knew what they would do—every experienced horse person would tell you that. Horses were unpredictable. Dangerous.

The fact that she didn't like horses hadn't stopped her from riding, though. She couldn't avoid it—it was too much a part of a ranch kid's life. She'd ridden fences with her mom and dad, ridden after stray calves, helped drive herds of cattle up to high pastures in the summer. She was a good rider, but not expert like Alison, or passionate like Meg. Riding a horse was just a way to get from one place to another. Personally, she'd rather drive a truck.

But they *did* need a better place to board Shadow.

There were no horses in sight, just tire tracks in the snow leading to the house and barn. Becky wondered if the ranch was still operating, with all the housing developments surrounding it. Above the barn's low roofline, she could see the Rockies, with the afternoon sun sliding down behind them. Becky found herself walking up the lane. Mustang Mountain Ranch was up there in those snow-covered mountains, but it felt very far away.

The door of the large riding arena stood partly open. Becky walked toward it, wondering what she would find inside.

CHAPTER 4

SARA AND ROB

There was just one horse in the arena, a big palomino. Becky froze. The horse looked like the dangerous horse of her nightmares. He was pale yellow, like butter, with a long golden mane and tail and a white blaze on his nose.

Walking the big horse around the ring was a girl wearing a brace on her left leg. She stopped when she saw Becky in the doorway.

"Hi, come on in. What can I do for you?"

The girl was older, maybe seventeen or eighteen. She was a human version of her horse, with long blonde hair tied back in a ponytail like Meg's. As she got closer, Becky saw that her eyes were a vivid blue, not a soft grayish blue like Meg's, but a blue that made you stare, it was so bright.

"I—I saw your sign," Becky stammered. "From the school bus." She pointed back to the road.

The girl's forehead knit in a puzzled frown. She looked Becky up and down, from her boots to her ski jacket to her backpack.

"I'm not sure I understand."

"We need—that is, my cousin needs—a place to board her horse."

"I see." The blonde girl smiled and nodded. "My name's Sara Kelly, by the way," she introduced herself, holding out her hand.

Becky stared. "I've heard your name—you're that champion barrel racer, aren't you?" She shook Sara's hand. "I'm Becky Sandersen. We just moved here from New York. At least, my cousin did. I've been living in New York with her to go to school, but my family lives up on a government ranch at Mustang Mountain."

"This sounds a bit confusing." Sara grinned. "Do you mind if we keep walking while you fill me in? I stiffen up if I stand too long in the cold." She glanced at her injured leg.

"How did you hurt yourself?" Becky had to ask.

"Oh, I was barrel racing on Sunny here and fell. Tore the ligaments in my knee and had surgery. It's healing, but it's slow."

"I'm sorry." Becky quickly fell into place beside her. They circled the cold ring, their breath puffing out in white clouds. "He's a—very tall horse," she added, looking over at Sunny.

"Yes, he's a big beautiful boy, but he's getting fat without enough exercise. He should be ridden every day, but with me out of commission, there's nobody else to do it." Sunny snorted and nuzzled Sara's shoulder.

"My cousin's horse needs more exercise, too," Becky said. "But she's not getting fatter. She's losing weight."

"That's not good. Any idea what's wrong?"

Becky paused. It was a long story. She tried to make it short. "My cousin Alison adopted Shadow at a wild horse auction in Wyoming last fall. She got trucked to New York and then all the way back here when Alison's parents split up. We've got her at a small stable. There are no other horses there right now, and she's not really used to that."

"That could be her problem, all right," Sara said, giving Becky a sympathetic glance. "We could board the mare here if it would help."

Just then, a small door at the end of the arena opened and a boy came through. As he walked toward them, Becky noticed that he was taller than Sara, and thinner.

"This is my brother, Rob," Sara said.

Rob nodded at Becky but didn't smile. He had the same blue eyes as his sister. In fact, their faces looked so much alike they could have been twins.

"There's a call for you," he said to Sara. "I think it's that lawyer guy again."

A red flush rose into Sara's cheeks as she handed the lead rope to Rob. "Here. Hold Sunny. I'll get rid of him fast enough!"

She limped off toward the door, swinging her brace out to the side to make better speed.

Rob shrugged. "Won't do any good," he muttered, rubbing Sunny's forehead. "We're all out of luck on this ranch, aren't we, fella?"

He glanced down at Becky. "I didn't see a car outside. How did you get here?"

"Off the school bus," Becky said, realizing how ridiculous that sounded. "I mean, our bus was passing your lane, and I saw your sign, and I just … hopped off."

Rob threw back his head and laughed. "I like that," he said. "Just an impulse, right?"

Becky had grown up with young men on ranches—cowboys with rough hands and a rough sense of humor. She'd learned to take their teasing and give it back. And she was not overly impressed by blue eyes under the rim of a cowboy hat. But this boy's eyes were kind, not teasing. His hair was light, like his sister's, cut short around his ears, his skin so pale it almost seemed you could see through it.

"Where do you live?" he asked.

"Down there," Becky pointed. "In one of the new developments."

She thought she saw him wince. "How were you planning to get home?"

"I guess I didn't think about that." Suddenly she wanted to explain why she was there. "Were you ever with somebody who was driving you crazy and you had to get away or you were going to strangle them?" she blurted.

Rob chuckled and started walking with the horse. "Plenty of times," he admitted. "In fact, that's pretty much the story of my life." He looked at her again with his serious blue eyes. "Do you have a bossy older sister, too?"

"No, she's my cousin," Becky said. "Is Sara bossy?"

"She wouldn't say so. She would just say she's always right!"

Becky burst out laughing. "That's exactly like my cousin Alison."

"Then I guess we have something in common." Rob smiled shyly at her. "What did you say your name was?"

"Becky, Becky Sandersen." Becky felt something inside her wobble at the look in his eyes. She suddenly felt like she was floating. Her ears rang and the colors in the dim arena grew brighter.

Sara was coming back, limping more slowly, but with the flush of anger still in her cheeks. "We have to go to town," she told Rob.

She turned to Becky. "If your cousin wants to board her horse here, have her come and take a look."

"I will," Becky promised. "I'll try to bring her."

Rob's eyes lit up. "A boarder?"

"I'll tell you all about it," Sara said briskly. "We've got to go. Nice meeting you."

"Maybe we can give Becky a lift home," Rob said, smiling again, "and she can tell me herself."

"Fine. Go warm up the truck, will you? I'll put Sunny away."

"Sure, big sister. Come on, Becky Sandersen."

Becky felt her knees shaking as she followed Rob to the pickup. If she could talk Alison into moving Shadow to Twin Rocks, she'd see him a lot.

*

Later, Becky had a chance to e-mail Meg.

Meg, URGENT! I have to tell somebody! DON'T TELL ALISON! I've met this guy, his name is Rob, and he makes me feel like I've never felt about anybody. I have to see him again, somehow. He doesn't go to my school—he lives in a different district. He's older, sixteen or seventeen, maybe. Anyway, he drives. It's so crazy, the way we met. I saw the sign to his ranch, Twin Rocks, and just walked up the lane to the barn like I knew where I was going (it would be a great place to board Shadow!). As soon as I saw Rob, it was like looking through a rainbow. I love the way he smiles at me. Is this how you feel about Thomas Horne?

Please e-mail me!
Becky

Meg answered:

That's exactly how I feel about Thomas, but I guess he doesn't feel the same way. He hasn't answered any of my e-mails in a long time. I guess guys forget. Oh well, someday I'll get over him. Are you going to board Shadow at Rob's ranch?

Becky shot back:

Don't give up on Thomas—there must be a reason he hasn't written. Maybe he went away to school, like I did.

I don't know if Alison will agree to move Shadow to Twin Rocks. Anyway, I'm afraid that once Rob sees Alison, that's the last time he'll ever look at me.

And Meg, finally:

Try not to stress over Alison! And thanks for the advice about Thomas. I'll try again. Got to go.

love you,
Meg

Becky deleted the messages in case Alison saw them. Poor Meg. She had met Thomas Horne at Mustang Mountain the summer before and fallen for him like a lovesick calf. Meg isn't the kind who gives her heart easily, and neither am I, Becky thought. Not like Alison, who throws herself at anything halfway cute and male. Wait until she claps eyes on Rob! Maybe I shouldn't even tell her about Twin Rocks. She paced the room with her long stride and stared out the window at the snowy night. Streetlights lit the snow-covered roofs of the new houses. It looked like a toy town.

Shadow needs a better boarding stable, Becky thought. I might not love horses, but I know them, and I know it's cruel to leave Shadow in that lonely cramped stall!

Before she fell asleep in the room she shared with Alison, Becky found herself thinking about Sara and Rob and wondering: If Sara needs someone to exercise Sunny, why doesn't Rob ride him?

CHAPTER 5

ALISON IN THE SADDLE

Becky started working on getting Shadow to Twin Rocks the next morning.

That wasn't easy. Alison hadn't spoken to her all night.

"I don't know what you thought you were doing!" she snapped as they walked down the hallway at school. "Why did you just jump off the bus and disappear like that?"

The hall was crowded and noisy. Becky had to shout to make herself heard.

"It doesn't matter why," she pleaded, "just listen. I found a great ranch where you could board Shadow. It's near our house, and the people seem nice. I met this girl ... Sara. She's a barrel racer."

"A rodeo rider?" Alison sneered. "Honestly, how hick can this place get?"

"Not all barrel racing is at rodeos," Becky hurried on. "And Sara Kelly is famous."

"Oh, really? I'll bet she wears fringed satin shirts and a great big silver buckle."

"Alison, you're such a snob!" Becky felt her cheeks flare. How dare Alison make fun of western dress.

"And you're so, so *impulsive*! I can't believe you just walked into somebody's place, off the road like that."

"I didn't. I'm trying to tell you. They had a sign advertising boarding for horses."

"I don't want to hear about it," Alison announced huffily.

"But, Alison, you need a better place to keep Shadow. You know you do."

Alison ignored her. "And then you get a ride home with a stranger! Don't you realize what could have happened to you?"

"This is Horner Creek, not New York." Becky wanted to scream.

"As if you needed to remind me." Alison raised her eyebrows at the hordes of students milling around them. "If you want to know the truth, every time I look at Shadow I think about the fight my parents had when she arrived from Wyoming. If I had never adopted Shadow, my parents would still be together and I'd still be living in New York, not this … zoo."

Becky looked hard at her cousin. "Okay, if that's how you feel." She shrugged. "But I'm going back to Twin Rocks Ranch anyway. I liked Sara and her brother. I'll have to make up some kind of reason why we aren't bringing Shadow to board—I mean, besides you being so pigheaded!"

Alison swiveled around like a satellite dish. "The famous barrel racer has a brother? How old is he?"

Here it comes, Becky sighed to herself. Alison's boy radar. Why did I ever say anything about Rob? Now she'll never rest until she gets every last detail out of me.

*

Rob wasn't there when they got to Twin Rocks after school that day.

"He had a doctor's appointment," Sara told Becky. "I'm afraid he won't be able to drive you home after you've had a look around."

"That's okay, we can walk to a bus stop," said Becky, swallowing her disappointment.

Alison marched into the arena as if she owned the ranch. She has no idea of good manners, Becky thought, embarrassed for her cousin. She walks in here like it was Bloomingdale's instead of someone's home.

"It's a nice place," Alison announced as they walked down the center hall of the spacious barn. She glanced at Sara. "Do you and your brother live here by yourselves?"

Becky could feel herself blushing. It's none of your business! she thought.

"Yes, we do." A brief shadow flickered across Sara's face. "My parents left it to us, and we have an uncle who helps out sometimes. My dad used to breed champion quarter horses and my mother showed them." She paused and looked around. "There's just a few old horses left now, and Sun Glow, my barrel racing horse. So we have lots of room for boarders."

Becky glanced sympathetically at her. Sara and Rob had lost both their parents when they were so young! She wondered what had happened to them.

Sara stopped at Sunny's stall and shook her head. "He's been cribbing again." She pointed to where the palomino had been chewing the wood of his stall and then turned to Becky and Alison. "Poor Sunny, he's so bored. I don't suppose either of you feels like a ride?"

Becky wanted to ask why Rob didn't ride him, but she bit her tongue. It wasn't her business, and besides, she didn't want to look overly interested in Rob.

"I'll ride him," Alison offered, shrugging. "He looks like fun."

Sara beamed with gratitude. "That's great. He might be a bit frisky after such a long layoff—are you sure you can manage?"

"I think so," Alison said sweetly, rolling her eyes at Becky. As if, her expression said, I couldn't handle a barrel horse after all the experience I've had with hot-headed horses.

Why didn't *I* offer to ride him? Becky thought irritably as she followed Alison and Sara to the tack room. But she knew the answer. The palomino brought back terrifying memories of falling off a horse.

A few minutes later, Alison was circling the indoor ring on Sunny's back.

"She's a beautiful rider!" Sara exclaimed, watching Alison's confident handling of the horse. "Look at the two of them—don't they look great?"

"Sure do," Becky muttered. Alison's slender straight body with her cap of dark hair contrasted perfectly with the golden horse. Sunny reached out into a smooth lope, clearly happy with his new rider.

As they came around even with them, Becky was startled to see the smile on Alison's face. It wasn't the sarcastic grimace she usually wore these days. Alison looked genuinely happy!

"He's wonderful," she sang out, pulling Sunny up in front of them. "Great gait, like he's floating!"

"You should see him gallop flat out around the barrels." Sara was glowing with pride. "He's the best barrel horse I've ever had."

"This horse could do anything." Alison leaned forward and stroked Sunny's neck. "Want a bit more, big guy? Sure, let's go!"

They set off around the ring, once more in perfect harmony.

"Where did Alison learn to ride like that?" Sara asked.

"She was a dressage champion," Becky said, trying not to sound too bitter. "English riding."

"That explains it." Sara nodded. "Sunny was trained English. Look at them go! You know, I'd board her horse for free if she'd come every day and ride Sunny like that."

Becky felt her heart sink. It's so typical of Alison to horn in on everything that matters to me, she thought. She wouldn't have cared about Sara or her horse, wouldn't have had anything to do with them, if she didn't know it would bug me.

CHAPTER 6

Rob's Secret

Becky's heart felt heavier when the barn door opened and Rob appeared.

He didn't even look at her.

He stopped short when he saw Alison circling the ring, as if stung by the sight.

Love at first glance, Becky thought miserably. I'll bet he's thinking he's never seen anything so beautiful in his life.

Rob turned to his sister. "Who's that riding Sun Glow?"

"That's Alison Chant. She's Becky's cousin." Sara never took her eyes from her horse.

"Oh, hi." There was that shy smile again. Rob took a couple of steps toward Becky and said in a low voice, "Is this the cousin who's always right?"

"You can see for yourself." Becky motioned to Alison. "She rides like a dream, too."

Rob shrugged. "So does my sister, when she isn't wearing a knee brace. It's no big deal."

Becky felt a bubble of relief rise inside her. So Rob wasn't carried away by the vision of Alison on horseback. It sounded like he wasn't impressed by his sister's riding, either. "Don't you ride Sunny?" she asked him point-blank.

Rob sighed deeply. "Not if I can help it."

Becky felt giddy. "Really?"

"That's right. But it's kind of my dark secret, so don't tell anyone, will you?" Rob was still smiling, but his eyes were serious.

"I won't. I understand." Becky felt like singing. No one, not even Meg, had understood how you could be a ranch kid and not love riding. But Rob did.

Alison had swung out of the saddle and was leading Sun Glow toward them. Sara limped beside her. The two of them were laughing and talking like old friends.

"This is my little brother, Rob," Sara introduced Rob to Alison. "Rob, this is Alison, Becky's—"

"Cousin, I know," Rob said, holding out his hand to Alison. "Hi."

"Hi, Rob," Alison said. Becky could tell by the tilt of Alison's head and the sparkle in her eye that she was impressed. Glancing at Rob, she could see the tips of his ears getting red. The vision of Alison up close was even better than far off. Perfect features, perfect smile. Wait till

42

she gets to work on him, Becky thought. She didn't know many guys who could resist Alison when she poured on the charm. And she was pouring it on now. "I'm so glad I've found you," she paused, "and this terrific ranch so close to Horner Creek."

"Alison's going to bring her horse here to board," Sara told Rob. "Isn't that great?"

"You are?" Becky blurted. She could feel anger rising in her like a storm.

"I think it's a great idea," Alison said coolly. "Don't you?"

Becky gaped at her. How totally typical of Alison to decide in a blink and then take credit for the idea! Both Sara and Rob smiled gratefully at Alison, glad to have the extra income from boarding Shadow. Alison looked just like her Grandmother Chant at that moment. Like a smug self-satisfied cat.

"Yes," Becky choked, "it's a very good idea."

That night, soaking in a hot bath, Alison relived the pleasure of her ride on Sunny. It was the first time since leaving New York that she'd felt truly happy. Up there on that big horse, circling the arena, she'd forgotten for a moment the misery of being an outcast at school, the prickly loneliness of not fitting in. I'll go back, she thought. I'll go back and ride Sunny whenever I can. He's a great horse—it's almost like riding Duchess again …

She sank lower in the tub as a wave of sadness

washed over her. Duchess—her beautiful champion—sold last fall and shipped off before Alison had a chance to say good-bye. I'll never forgive my father for selling her, Alison thought, suddenly angry. No wonder my mother is divorcing him.

She stood up and reached for a towel. Wrapped in white terrycloth, Alison frowned at herself in the bathroom mirror. What's wrong? she asked her reflection. No zits, no bulges, no bad hair. So why does Rob Kelly act like I'm about as interesting as a barn door? I can understand those Horner Creek kids ignoring me. They wouldn't know someone special if they tripped over her. But Rob saw me ride. Why didn't I make an impression on him?

Alison lowered her chin and batted her long eyelashes. Am I slipping? No, not possible. Maybe it's Rob. Maybe there's something wrong with him!

✱

The following week, at ten-thirty Wednesday night, Becky and Meg were on the computer to each other. It was two hours later in New York than Calgary. Becky knew she was keeping Meg up, but the only time she had privacy was when Alison spent an hour in the bathroom before bed.

Becky wrote:

I think Twin Rocks is going to work out for Shadow. She's settling in and starting to put on weight again. Alison's working on Rob, but so far he's not falling all over her the way most guys do. Of course, she's furious about this and keeps trying to get his attention, showing off by riding his sister's barrel racing horse. Hey, maybe I'm jealous?

Meg answered:

Hay is for horses. Ha–ha. And speaking of horses, I'm glad to hear Shadow's doing better. Is Alison thinking about training her yet? I've been working with Patch, and she's doing really well. Terri-Lyn did a good job starting her under saddle. I'm lungeing her before I ride to get her supple and then doing short rides in the ring. Can't wait to hack her around the Blue Barn trails. Must go now. Big math test tomorrow and it's past midnight.

love you,
Meg

Alison came bouncing out of the bathroom just as Becky was signing off. "Are you e-mailing Meg?" She peered over Becky's shoulder. "Move, I want to send her a message."

"It's late, she has to study," Becky protested, but Alison had already shoved her out of the chair and was clicking away at the keyboard.

"This won't take long. Do you mind giving *me* some privacy for a change?" She gave Becky an irritated glance over her shoulder. "I haven't talked to Meg in a long time."

Becky sighed and took her turn in the bathroom while Alison wrote to Meg.

Meg! I'm riding the most amazing horse. His name is Sunny, and he's a palomino barrel racing horse. A real champion. Riding him almost makes me forget how miserable I am out here. Mom's still working all the time. The kids at school act like I don't exist, and Becky's so into Rob that she walks around in a daze! I keep remembering our good times at Blue Barn, and thinking about how my life has gone wrong ever since I lost Duchess last fall. Anyway, I just wanted to write and tell you that I miss you like crazy. Please write back.

your lonesome pal,
Al

Meg got Alison's message as she was about to turn off the computer for the night. She shook her head. Poor Alison! She only called herself Al when she was feeling really lonely. But Meg was tired. She'd write back tomorrow. In the meantime, she just wished Alison and Becky could work things out.

CHAPTER 7

BLOWUP!

"What's the matter with Rob?" Alison whispered. They were at Twin Rocks. Becky was brushing Shadow, and Rob had just left to get her a bucket of oats.

"What do you mean?" Becky's brush froze on Shadow's withers, just for a second, and the horse twitched as though she caught the current of emotion. "Nothing's the matter with him."

"I know you think he's purrfect," Alison drawled out the word, "but he's so pale. I mean, for a person who lives out here in the sunny west and works on a ranch, he's awfully pasty looking. And he keeps going to the doctor." Alison stepped out of Shadow's stall.

"So? Just because Rob isn't falling for you doesn't make him sick." Becky went on with her brushing of

Shadow's neck and belly, but she knew she was making the horse nervous. Shadow pinned back her ears.

Alison shrugged. "I'm just asking a question. Maybe Rob's got something wrong with him. Maybe that's why he never rides Sunny for Sara."

Becky ground her teeth. "What if he just doesn't like to ride?"

Alison cocked her head to one side like an eager bird. "You mean, like you?" she asked. "He's a real soul mate, I suppose that's what you're thinking. Honestly, you're so pathetic."

"What do you mean by that?" Becky's voice rose. She could feel the anger flame in her cheeks.

"I mean it's so obvious you like him, but you'll never admit it. You always act so superior because you never get crushes on guys, and I do. Now you're crazy about Skinny Rob, but you're not going to say anything."

"Not to you," Becky declared. Alison was disgusting. How *dare* she?

Rob had come back with the bucket of feed. He stopped and stared, not at them, but at Shadow. "Step away," he said in a low voice to Becky.

"What's the matter?" Becky dropped her hands.

"Look at Shadow. Something's spooked her. You'd better get out of the stall."

Becky took a step back. Now she could see Shadow's eye, hard and rimmed with white. She remembered the stories about Shadow at the mustang adoption center last fall—how she'd kicked and lashed out at her captors, fought against them until she'd made herself sick. Shadow shifted her weight to her hindquarters and jerked up her head. Becky's fear came rushing back. She was in a stall with a dangerous horse. The image of flashing, pounding hooves filled her brain. She froze.

Rob opened the stall door, reached for her arm and yanked her through the narrow opening. He grabbed the door latch and rammed it shut. The latch made a harsh, grating sound.

It was a familiar and hated sound to Shadow—the sound of the squeeze chute at the adoption center when they'd tried to freeze-brand and vaccinate her after her capture. At the unexpected noise, Shadow exploded. She lashed out with her hind hooves, rattling the stall's sturdy timbers. Her front hooves flashed as she reared and kicked at the door. With each thump, Becky's heart pounded louder.

"She's just scared!" Alison cried. "You've got to go back in there and calm her down."

Becky feared that if she went into the stall now, Shadow would attack her. "You go," she choked.

"I wouldn't," Rob said quietly. "Wait till she calms down."

"But we're undoing all Cousin Terri-Lyn's work." Alison stamped her foot. "If Shadow thinks she can blow up in her stall and get us to leave, we'll never be able to work with her."

"And if you go in there now, you might get hurt," Rob said. "What set her off?"

"I don't know." Alison gave Becky a sideways glance. "I think Becky was making her nervous. We were arguing."

Becky glared at Alison.

Rob looked from one to the other. "Somebody must have been awful mad to work up a horse that way. Maybe it was something else."

"I don't know why Becky got so mad." Alison shrugged. "I only said—"

"It's my fault," Becky almost shouted. "It doesn't matter what we were fighting about. We won't do it again, not around Shadow anyway." She stood back from the stall so Shadow couldn't feel the waves of rage and fear sweeping over her. She'd strangle Alison if she told Rob she liked him.

The mustang was still rolling her eyes and pawing at her shavings, but she had stopped kicking.

"See, Shadow's okay. She just misses her friend, Patch," Alison said. "Her nose has started running again, like it did before we brought her here. I think she's lonely. Can we put her in with Sun Glow?"

"My sister wouldn't like that." Rob shook his head. "Sunny is her baby."

"Are there any other animals around?" Becky asked. She was struggling to regain her composure. "Up at Mustang Mountain, we sometimes put a cat or a goat in with a difficult horse. It seems to relax them."

"Hey, that's a great idea." Rob beamed. "We might have just the friend for Shadow." He led the way to the end of the barn, where a small mule was stabled. The mule had big ears and a scruffy coat the color of mouse fur.

"Meet Chompster," Rob told them. "This mule's so stubborn and ornery I don't know why we keep him. He doesn't bite, but he'll chew anything he can get his teeth on, including your hat, if you let him." He leaned over the stall door to scratch Chompster between the ears. "He was kind of a pet of my dad's."

Becky saw Rob squint hard and wondered if he was missing his father.

"Are you thinking of putting this mule in with my horse?" Alison was peering at Chompster, her hands on her hips. "I don't think …"

"Maybe they'll take to each other," said Rob. "Chompster's been lonely since Dad went. Shadow is sure lonely. She's been separated from her herd and lost her friend—she's mad and confused after all the changes in her life."

Becky could see the wisdom in this. And she could hear in Rob's voice that he knew about loneliness himself. Maybe someday he'd tell her what had happened to his parents.

"I hope you know what you're doing," Alison muttered as Rob put on the mule's halter and led him down the barn.

"We'll just put him in the next stall at first," Rob suggested. He opened the door of the box stall next to Shadow and shoved Chompster hard on the rump. The mule gave a loud "hee-haw" and allowed himself to be pushed inside.

Shadow looked through the bars separating the stalls to see what had made that strange noise.

Chompster brayed again and stuck his head up to meet Shadow's inquisitive nose.

Shadow bobbed her head a couple of times, as if saying hello.

"We should leave them alone to get acquainted," Rob said. "If it works out, we'll put them together in the big box stall."

Becky hung back as they watched the horse and the mule make friends, feeling ashamed for losing control of her temper around Shadow. The mustang had grown up in the wild—far from human beings. She had no way of knowing the difference between anger directed at her and at a person. Alison was right—they were undoing all the work done trying to get Shadow to trust people.

Becky managed to get on the computer that night to write to Meg. At the end of the long message, she wrote:

Alison insists there's something wrong with Rob. She says he's too pale for somebody who spends so much time outside, and too thin. His skin is light, almost like you could see through it. And he has bruises on his arms. Also, he doesn't ride Sara's horse, even though Sara can't ride because of her torn knee ligament. I think it's just because he doesn't like riding, but Alison insists there's some other reason. I know she just says these things to bug me, and maybe she's mad because Rob isn't falling at her feet. But I have to admit, she's got me worried.

Meg replied:

Don't let Alison get under your skin. That's what she wants, to make you look bad in front of Rob. IGNORE HER and just be yourself. And don't forget, even though she drives you crazy, she has problems of her own. She hates being snubbed at school, and she misses home.

It's probably nothing, but if you want, I can check those symptoms of Rob's on the special medical network my mom subscribes to. Say the word.

Becky wrote back:

Thanks, Meg. That's a good idea to check Rob's symptoms on the Net. But don't bother to use your mom's service. I can use a computer at school. Too dangerous to do it here—can't count on privacy! What would I do without you?

love, hugs,
B

Becky climbed into bed, thinking of Rob with a bitter ache. Did he like her, or was he just being friendly? Did he know how she felt about him? Becky hoped he didn't. She didn't want to lose him as a friend. Rob was a lot more important to her than Josh, a cowboy she'd had a crush on in Wyoming. Josh was good-looking and nice, but Rob understood what she was thinking. He seemed to see right into her. Alison, with all her teasing, was right. Becky did think of Rob as a kind of soul mate.

CHAPTER 8

BARREL RACE

Within a few days, it was clear that Shadow and Chompster were going to be friends. Rob turned them out every day in the same paddock, and they shared a roomy box stall at the far end of the barn.

"Look at Shadow," Alison sighed. "She's so much happier. Her nose has quit running."

"Just keep your eye on Chompster," Rob laughed. "He didn't get his name for nothing."

When Rob smiled, Becky noticed, his eyes always stayed serious. It was as if nothing reached the sadness inside.

Sara was studying Shadow. "You know, your mustang might make a good barrel horse, if she likes to run."

"Do you think so?" Alison glanced at Sara. "Isn't she kind of small?"

"She's compact, and she has strong straight legs under her. Some of the best barrel horses aren't very big." Sara smiled at Alison. "You've never been to a barrel race, have you?"

Alison shook her head. "I've seen it on TV."

"That's not the same as the real thing. There's an indoor race at Pine Valley later in March. Maybe we should go."

Becky saw Alison smiling like she'd be thrilled to go to a barrel race. Hypocrite! She wasn't really interested in rodeo—she was a snob about western riding in general.

Rob turned to Becky. "Would you like to go?"

"Sure." She shrugged. Does it matter what I'd like? she thought. We're all going to end up doing what Alison wants. But it's still nice of him to ask.

The Pine Valley barrel race was held in an indoor arena because it was still too cold for outdoor events. The big arena floor was layered with clay and sand. Becky, Alison and Rob made their way slowly up into the stands, waiting for Sara to maneuver her brace over the benches.

"This is fine," she finally said, plunking down on a metal bench. "I like to sit opposite the first two barrels."

"Tell me how it works," Alison asked Rob, giving him her "I'm so dumb and you're so smart" look. Becky bit her lip. Alison was so obvious, but it always seemed to work on guys!

"Pretty simple," Rob said. "You see those three barrels set up—two opposite each other at the beginning of the race and a third, the point barrel, at the far end. Horses and riders usually run *right* around the first barrel, *left* around the second, *left* around the third and then ride like fury back to the electric eye beam, when the clock stops. Races are won by fractions of a second. A good barrel horse knows how to run fast, circle close to the barrels without knocking them over and then run a real straight line back to the finish. You'll see."

"You like this event?" Becky was surprised at the enthusiasm in his voice.

"I like watching it." Rob nodded. "It's exciting and it's a race. There are no points for style or grace or the size of the horse. Speed counts, and the clock doesn't lie. Unless of course there's a penalty added to the time."

"Oh." Alison changed the subject. "Sara's a wonderful rider, when she's not hurt, isn't she?"

"The very best." Rob nodded again and went back to staring at the ring. "Before her accident she'd already qualified for this year's Calgary Stampede rodeo—she could have won fifty thousand dollars in the barrels."

They looked over at Sara, sitting with her injured leg outstretched. "This must be really hard on her," Alison murmured. "I'm happy to ride Sunny for her, just to keep him in condition, but why don't you ever ride him?"

"I don't ride my sister's horse."

There was something in Rob's voice that made Becky glance at him quickly, but his face was a mask. He's used to hiding his feelings, Becky thought, but there's something wrong here. The action in the ring drew her attention away. This was the sweepstakes event, with all the top riders from each division entered.

The first rider was a small girl with a flying brown ponytail, and a muscular brown horse that seemed to dance around the barrels. Sometimes the horse and rider were at such a steep angle in the turns it seemed only their speed kept them from crashing to the ground.

"Wow!" Alison gasped. "She's good!"

"That's Melissa Dale. She's only eleven, and one of the best riders around," Rob told them. "She made a good run. I'll bet her time is under 16 seconds."

Alison's eyes were shining as she turned to Rob. "That doesn't look hard—it looks like fun! Do you think Sara would let me practice barrel racing on Sunny?"

"She might," Rob said. "You never know with Sara."

"That would be fantastic!" Alison cried.

Becky gulped down the words she wanted to say. For Alison to talk like that, after putting down western riding so much, was completely phony!

The announcer came back on. Rob was right. Melissa had ridden the course in 15.9 seconds.

"Let's go stand by the rail," Alison urged. "I want to see the action up close."

"I guess so," Rob said with a glance at Becky. "You coming, too?"

Becky grinned. "Sure." If Alison thought she was getting Rob off by herself, she could go rope a steer.

The next rider was a man in a cowboy hat, mounted on a large chestnut mare. "I don't like the way this guy rides," Rob muttered. "He's been warned about overusing his spurs and the whip."

"He must be three times older than Melissa!" Alison exclaimed. "How come they're riding against each other?"

"It's the sweepstakes." Rob shrugged. "Best ride wins. Don't worry about Melissa. Kids often beat old pros."

The horse and rider galloped from behind the chutes, spun round the first barrel, cut a clean line to the second, rounded it and headed for the third barrel.

Becky saw what Rob meant. As they rounded the third barrel, the rider put the whip to his horse. When he crossed the finish line, he was a few tenths of a second faster than Melissa.

"But that's not fair!" Alison's pale face was wrathful. "Melissa would have beaten him if he hadn't used the whip. Isn't it illegal?"

"No. Depends how you use the whip whether it's cruel to the horse." Rob's eyes narrowed. "Jake Grady is a bully. If he keeps it up, he'll be banned from the barrel racing association."

"I wish Melissa had beaten him," Alison muttered. "It's not fair."

Another horse and rider came flying through the alley. The announcer's voice cut through the crowd noise.

"It's Stacey Johannsen on Danny's Choice. She's got a

good fast start, set up for the first barrel … a little too tight … oh! too bad, she knocked over the barrel for a penalty of five seconds."

The rider finished the course and the time was announced. The penalty was added for a total of 22 seconds.

"Too bad for Stacey," Rob said. "That'll put her out of the standings."

A man in a green shirt hopped over the rails and set up the fallen first barrel.

"So Jake Grady's time is still the best," Alison said. "I wish someone would beat him!"

"You might get your wish." Rob grinned. "This next rider will give him a run for his money."

CHAPTER 9

CRASH LANDING

At the end of the ring, they saw a slender girl lean forward on her dark bay horse, ready for a quick start.

"The next rider is Diane Turcotte on Dark Diamond," the announcer bellowed.

"Diane has a good horse," Rob told them.

Diane rode like she was part of her horse, her elbows tight to her body, her weight forward. They headed toward the first barrel, the one closest to Becky, Alison and Rob, standing at the rail.

All of a sudden, Dark Diamond stumbled, in full flight, going into the turn. Diane came flying at them, over her horse's head. Becky could see the surprise on her face before she crashed into the rails with a sickening thump and slumped to the arena floor like a broken doll.

There was a single gasp from the crowd, a split second of silence and then everyone was yelling and moving at once.

Dark Diamond was hobbling around the ring. People ran to catch him. A doctor and two stretcher bearers converged on Diane's still body, while someone straightened the fallen barrel.

"Poor girl." Becky squeezed her eyes shut. Once more she was reliving her own fall—the terrible feeling of slamming to the ground.

"Poor horse." Alison's eyes were on Dark Diamond. "What happened? What made him go down like that?"

Sara came up behind them. "Rob, quick, go see if there's anything wrong with the footing where they fell. Hurry! Before it gets messed up with so many people milling around."

"You think there's something wrong with the footing?" Rob looked worried.

"Somebody should look." Sara sounded frantic. "If only I didn't have this dumb brace on!"

"What did you see?" Rob put a hand on his sister's arm.

Sara's cheeks were almost as pale as Rob's. "Diane's horse fell exactly the same way Sunny fell."

"It was awful." Becky shivered. "She crashed into the rail, right in front of us."

They were carrying Diane out of the arena, and someone had managed to catch Dark Diamond and lead him away. The loudspeaker was playing tinny music. A large tractor with a rake behind it had come out to drag the arena dirt smooth.

Sara leaned over the rail to peer at the dirt where Dark Diamond had stumbled. His hoofprints, along with many others, were about to disappear under the teeth of the rake.

"Stay here," Sara said. "I'm going to talk to the organizers. Try to get them to stop the race."

"Would they go on with it, after the accident?" Becky asked.

"Probably. Falls are part of racing," said Rob. But he was looking after his sister as if bothered about something. "It *is* weird that Sunny and Dark Diamond fell the same way," he muttered.

"You still want to barrel race?" Becky threw over her shoulder at Alison. "You can see how dangerous it is."

"Every kind of racing is dangerous, like Rob says." Alison gave a careless toss of her head. "Hacking around a park is dangerous. You wouldn't ride at all if you're a sissy about falling."

Becky said nothing. She wasn't a sissy, but the smack of Diane hitting that rail and the sight of her crumpled on the arena floor had made her stomach churn.

"I'd better go find Sara," Rob said. "If I know my big sister, she's raising a stink." He took in both of them with his smile and headed for the announcer's stand.

Becky followed him with her eyes.

"He's dreamy, isn't he?" teased Alison. "Definitely the lean quiet type, with the emphasis on lean."

"Mind your own business," Becky snapped, annoyed at having been caught watching Rob.

"I guess I'll be seeing *a lot* of Rob." Alison tipped her head to one side, still teasing. "I'm going to spend all my spare time at Twin Rocks from now on. I think I'm going to take up barrel racing." She snorted with laughter. "Just think how much my Grandmother Chant would hate that! It's so *rough* and so *western!*"

Just think how much *I'd* hate it. Becky glared at her cousin. *I* found Twin Rocks. Me, not you. And now you act like the place was yours—you big fake!

Later, Sara came limping back, looking exhausted. "It's no use." She shook her head. "Barrel horses trip and stumble all the time, they say. We don't need a special investigation every time they do." She collapsed on the bench. "I still think there's something wrong. It was the *way* Dark Diamond stumbled going into the turn—it was exactly like Sunny's fall."

CHAPTER 10

RIDING LESSONS

"Mother, I want to take riding lessons again," Alison announced at breakfast a week later.

Her mother had been on a selling trip to the east coast. She was groggy from jet lag and lack of sleep. "Sounds okay," she muttered. "As long as they're not too expensive."

"Are we worried about money?" Alison gave her mother a challenging look.

"We're living on my salary now, not your father's. And the bit your father sends us doesn't come close to making up the difference." Marion Chant lifted her chin. "So, we have to watch our expenses." Becky had to hide a smile. The Chants' idea of cutting back was to buy shrimp instead of lobster.

"Well, I'm sure barrel racing lessons at Twin Rocks won't be too expensive," Alison muttered.

"Did you say … barrel racing?" Alison's mother choked on her coffee. "Like in a rodeo?"

Sitting across the table, Becky felt sorry for her aunt. Aunt Marion had invested a fortune in Alison's high-priced dressage lessons, another fortune on her horse and stable fees, fancy riding clothes and gear. At one time, she'd hoped Alison would become an Olympic rider. That dream seemed far away, and now Alison was talking about a kind of riding her mother couldn't even imagine.

"Barrel racing is more than rodeo, Mother," Alison said. "It's a serious sport. It's great, and having Sara Kelly as a teacher would be awesome."

"I don't think so," Marion said slowly, shaking her head. Becky thought her aunt looked very tired.

"Look, Mother, I have no friends, I'm going crazy in that boring school, and I hate this place!" Alison rose to her feet, her eyes flashing. "This is the first thing I've wanted to do besides lie in bed and cry since I got to Horner Creek! You keep telling me to adjust and try to fit in. Well, here's my chance!"

"All right!" Marion held up her hand. "All right. If the lessons aren't outrageously expensive, you can take them. As long as you don't expect me to buy you—one of those rodeo horses."

"Sara has a great horse that I've already been riding. She says I can learn on him. And I keep telling you, it's not all rodeo!"

"Becky, you're awfully quiet. What do you think of this?" her aunt asked. Becky saw how the lines around Marion Chant's mouth and eyes had deepened in the two and a half months since they'd come to Horner Creek.

"Sunny is a really nice horse. If you want to barrel race, I guess Twin Rocks is a good place to start." She left out the part about flying off horses and smacking into rails.

"Grandmother Chant will hate it," Alison added.

If she expected this to cheer up her mother, it didn't. Instead she got a long look from under dark eyebrows that were almost identical to her own. "You don't have to fight with your grandmother just because I do," she said. "And you may want her good wishes someday."

"You mean I might want her money!" Alison shot back. "But I don't."

Her mother smiled. "I'm glad you want to be independent of the Chant fortune, but I still wouldn't do things just to spite your grandmother."

"It's not spite! I want to try barrel racing. Is that so weird?"

"In my opinion, yes. But go ahead if you want to try it." Alison's mother shrugged in defeat. "When would lessons start?"

"Whenever I want. I'll be getting private tutoring."

Always the snob, Becky smiled to herself. Alison would be getting "private tutoring" because she was the only student Sara Kelly had!

✱

"I think I'll start next Saturday," Alison said later that night. "That way, I can have the whole day for my first lesson, not just after school."

"Are you going to take barrel racing lessons every day?" Becky asked, surprised.

"Well, maybe not *every* day." Alison shrugged. "But as often as I can. Why?"

"I was just wondering who's going to look after Shadow while you're racing around the barrels on Sunny." Becky twirled the belt from her dressing gown like a lariat. "You won't have any time for her."

"No, I guess not." Alison made a sour face at the mention of her mustang, and Becky knew it was because she'd already been neglecting Shadow while riding Sunny and hated to be reminded of that.

"Maybe you can take her over," Alison suggested. "You've been grooming her and handling her as much as I have."

"Not me." Becky shook her head. Since Shadow's blowup, she'd been nervous of close contact with the mustang. "Anyway, it's not just grooming and handling that Shadow needs. Someone should be training her." Becky flopped back on her bed. "Did you know that Meg is already riding Patch? She says Terri-Lyn did a good job starting her. But Shadow's so skittish I think somebody might have to start all over again with her."

"Rob will help you," Alison said with a sly look at Becky, "if you ask him."

So typical, Becky thought angrily. Just throw poor Shadow to anyone who'll take her—now that you're barrel racing crazy!

But she was right—Rob probably would help—he didn't seem to be nervous around Shadow, even if he didn't like horses much. And she would get to spend more time with him if they trained Shadow together. "Okay," she agreed. "I'll go to Twin Rocks after school tomorrow and ask Rob if he'll help with Shadow."

CHAPTER 11

Surprises

Becky felt like singing as she stepped off the school bus at the Twin Rocks sign the next day. It was the second of April and spring was in the air. A dry wind swept down from the mountains, and the last patches of snow were melting from the hollows.

As she hurried down the lane toward the barn, Becky hoped she would get a chance to be alone with Rob. She had dressed carefully that morning, new jeans and a green polar fleece jacket that looked good with her golden skin and dark blonde hair. She'd always dressed without thinking too much about it. Now it seemed important to wear something to catch Rob's eye. She knew he already liked her—as a friend. But she wanted him to see her as a girl.

Becky was surprised at herself. In the last two years, she'd watched Alison fall in love as if guys were potato chips and she couldn't resist just one more. And Meg had fallen like a cement block for Thomas last summer. But Becky honestly believed it wouldn't happen to her, at least not for a long time.

I thought I was cowboy-proof, Becky thought. She rubbed her stomach, where butterflies were doing a dance as she got closer to the barn. After all the older guys I've met on ranches, with their smelly socks and smart remarks, I thought I could never care about one of *them*. But Rob is different. He's not smelly. He's sensitive, and quiet, and his whole life isn't wrapped up with cattle and horses. Most of all, I like the way he smiles.

Thinking about Rob's smile made Becky's legs wobbly and numb. She couldn't walk fast enough to get to the end of that long lane. She hoped he would agree to help her with Shadow. Poor little mare, so unloved since this move to Horner Creek.

Nobody was in the arena, so Becky strode across the ring to the barn's connecting door. She could hear Rob working at the far end. He must be mucking out Shadow and Chompster's big stall. I could help, Becky thought. She grabbed a shovel and headed toward the stall.

But before she got very far, she stopped, flooded with disappointment. Rob wasn't alone. He was talking to someone.

"Now you listen, girl," she heard him say. "I know you're mad and confused, and you've gone through a lot of tough changes." He was talking in such a soft, loving voice that Becky was afraid she was interrupting something private. "I know that right now what you'd really like to do is kick me into the next creek."

"He's talking to Shadow," Becky whispered to herself. "*To a horse!*"

"There, girl, take it easy," Rob went on in his soothing voice. "I'm going to take you out for some real exercise. You've been cooped up too long. It's all right—Chompster's coming, too. It's a great day. The sun is shining, and you're going to love the pasture."

Becky took a few steps closer, not making a sound, not wanting to scare Shadow. She could just see Rob now, over the top of the stall. He was wearing a cowboy hat and had a halter in his hand.

Standing close to Shadow's side, he went on talking in that gentle, coaxing voice. Shadow was listening. Her left ear was swiveled to catch Rob's voice, and her eyes were soft as she turned to sniff the halter.

Becky felt a prickle of fear. Terri-Lyn had worked Shadow in the halter and bridle in Wyoming, but that was months ago. What would she do when Rob tried to put on a halter now?

But Rob easily slipped on the halter, talking to her all the time, patting and stroking the little paint's cheek and neck. Becky ducked into another stall so he wouldn't see her. Rob opened the stall door and led Shadow calmly toward the door at the far end. Chompster clomped after them, braying to be included in the outing.

Becky followed. Outside, she watched Rob unclip Shadow's lead rope and let her frisk away after the mule, who was trotting toward the far pasture fence.

Rob stood there with his hands in his pockets and his shoulders hunched up, watching them. "Hi, Rob," Becky said, forcing the words out, suddenly shy.

"Becky! Hi." Rob swung around and looked at her in surprise, his eyes as wide and blue as the spring sky.

"I didn't know you were coming out this afternoon," he said.

"I wanted—I thought I might spend some time with Shadow," she stammered. "Alison asked me to look after her—since she's going to be barrel racing."

"Oh, sorry." Rob frowned. "I wouldn't have turned her out if I'd known. It's just such a nice day."

"No, that's okay," Becky's words tumbled out. "I heard you talking to her. You're great with horses." She was longing to say she didn't understand—her theory about him not liking horses was evaporating like a puddle in the desert!

Rob grinned. "I've been thinking someone should start Shadow under saddle again." He gazed out at where she was grazing in the pasture. "She's a fine little mare. I'd hate to see her go wild again until she's only fit for dog food."

"Oh. I'm sure Alison would be happy if you got her used to being ridden again." Becky gulped. And it will save me from having to get on her back, she thought to herself. "So, you like training horses?" She had to ask.

"I should. I've been doing it as long as I can remember." Rob narrowed his eyes and kept them fixed on the horizon. "And I guess I always had a dream of working with my dad on this ranch, breeding and training quarter horses. But that's not going to happen."

"Your parents," Becky finally asked. "What happened?"

"Well, my mom got cancer and ... died. My dad was a lot older. He just lived another three months, then had a heart attack." Rob's face was completely neutral, as if he were talking about someone else's family, but Becky could hear the loss like an echo behind the words.

"I'm sorry" was the only thing she could think of saying.

"It was last year," Rob said, as if a year was a lifetime ago.

"But you still have the ranch." Becky looked around the pasture and buildings.

"Yes and no. It's ours, but Sara and I can't make a go of it ourselves. I've still got a couple of years of high school, and Sara wants to study to be a vet starting this fall. We should sell Twin Rocks to a developer and buy a cheaper spread up there." He gestured toward the mountains. "But this place is all tied up with the lawyers until Sara's twenty-one—three more years." He shrugged. "Meanwhile, we can hardly afford hay for the horses we've got. We were kind of counting on Sara's barrel racing winnings for cash to get us through the next while and pay university fees." He stopped suddenly and his pale cheeks flushed. "I shouldn't be telling you all this."

"It's all right." So that was what the lawyer thing was all about—when Sara had had to leave the first day Becky was at Twin Rocks. She cleared her throat. "Sara's getting her brace off. She'll be riding again soon, won't she?"

"Riding maybe, but not racing. And not in time for the Stampede. That's the big prize—fifty thousand dollars."

"Oh." He looked so miserable that Becky changed the subject. "Shadow seems to be enjoying herself out there. How were you planning to catch her?"

Rob's shoulders relaxed. "That's easy. I figure she'll follow Chompster back to the stall. I can always catch that greedy mule with food. He's a sucker for carrots."

Becky laughed with him, but the whole time she was thinking furiously, I'm so stupid, I was so wrong. Rob loves horses. He's as horse crazy as Meg, and he'd like to train a half-wild mustang, so he can't be afraid of them. Shadow will be in good hands! Better than mine.

But through Becky's whirl of emotions, she could hear the echo of a question—if he loves horses so much, why won't he ride Sunny?

*

When Becky got home, she had her answer to that question. There was a message from Meg.

"Can I see?" Alison begged, looking over Becky's shoulder as she sat at the computer.

"It's private," Becky growled.

"So, now you and Meg are having conversations behind my back. Nice."

"It doesn't concern you."

"Don't worry, I know how you two have your own little club that I'm not part of." Alison whirled out of the room.

Becky sighed as she opened Meg's message. She knew how much Alison hated being excluded from her friendship with Meg. If only she wouldn't be so sarcastic. It made you not care how she felt.

When she read Meg's e-mail, she was very glad Alison wasn't reading over her shoulder.

Hi Becky,

It's been weeks since you've said anything about Rob's being sick, and I was on Mom's network tonight, so I entered his symptoms. They match a condition called thrombocytopenia. That long word means your blood doesn't clot right. So you bruise easily and can bleed internally. Maybe Rob doesn't ride because, if he fell off, he could bleed into his joints, or hemorrhage. I'm really, really sorry. Do you think you should ask him about it?

Becky got up and locked the door, then wrote back to Meg.

Oh, Meggie, Rob seemed fine, so I forgot all about looking up his symptoms. Or maybe I just didn't want to know. But this all fits. His pale skin, the bruises on his arms. He is sick! Today he offered to start riding Shadow, but it's too dangerous. I've got to stop him! What am I going to do?

CHAPTER 12

FACING THE NEWS

Becky read Meg's message over and over, the words blazing at her from the screen. Alison had been right all along. Rob was sick! He might die!

No wonder he wouldn't ride Sunny for Sara. He couldn't take the risk, not even to help his sister earn the prize money they needed to keep the ranch going. But he loved horses—he wanted to be a horse breeder like his dad, *like my dad, too*, she thought. She had a vision of Rob at Mustang Mountain Ranch, working with the horses, keeping careful breeding records.

But it would never happen. Rob couldn't work on an isolated wilderness ranch—it was so far from the nearest hospital! And he might die before he was old enough to sell Twin Rocks and get a place of his own. Becky read

Meg's message once more. She didn't say anything about how long a person could live with thrombocytopenia. If only she could talk to Meg, but she couldn't call New York on Aunt Marion's line, especially now that her aunt was nervous about money.

Maybe Rob's future would depend on how well he looked after himself. Becky shuddered. Even if you never rode, working with horses could be dangerous. Her mother had been kicked in the spine while shoeing a horse and had broken a vertebra. A blow like that could kill Rob if it caused bleeding inside.

He would have to be especially careful around Shadow, Becky knew. He couldn't, he shouldn't, work with her. Wild horses were unpredictable, and the mare had already blown up once. A loud banging on the den door made her jump.

"Do you mind? I need to use the computer!"

Alison! Becky quickly deleted Meg's message and her reply, stood up and opened the door.

Alison glared at her. "Honestly, I've heard of locking the bathroom door, but this is ridiculous."

"Sorry, I was just doing some research."

"Sure you were. What did Meg have to say?"

"Not much." Becky shoved her hair behind her ears and tried to sound casual. "You know Meg."

"Liar. I know she wrote something that's upset you. I can tell by that flush in your cheeks. But keep your silly secrets, I don't care." Alison flopped into a chair. "How was Sickly Rob today?"

"What?" Did she know?

"Rob Kelly. Did you tell him you like him?"

Becky took a deep breath. Alison didn't know anything. She was just being her usual obnoxious self! "No, I didn't tell him. He was working with Shadow this afternoon," she said. "He turned her out in the pasture and he wants to start her under saddle again. He says we should try to keep her from getting wild again."

"How sweet of him. He's welcome to train her, if you don't want to." Alison gave a careless shrug.

Becky lost her temper. "Why did you bother adopting Shadow if you are just going to dump her?" she blazed.

"I'm not exactly *dumping* her ..." Alison started to protest.

"Well, what would you call it then? This is so typical of you! You get wildly excited about something and then drop it as soon as something else comes along. First it was dressage, then wild horses. I wonder how long this great fascination with barrel racing will last?"

"Just you wait and see!" Alison jumped up and did a dance step in the den. "Barrel racing is different. I knew it when I saw Melissa Dale ride. It's what I want to do, and I've got a champion to teach me and a champion horse to ride." She threw up her arms. "My first lesson's in two more days—it's going to be amazing!"

Saturday they took a bus as close to Twin Rocks as they could get and walked the rest of the way. Three barrels were already set up in the riding arena. Sara had Sunny saddled and ready.

Becky anxiously scanned Rob's face. Apart from looking a little paler than usual, he seemed okay. He gave her a special smile that wrung her heart.

"Ready to set the barrel racing world on fire?" he asked Alison.

"You bet." Alison took Sunny's reins from Sara.

She rode a couple of slow practice runs around the barrels as Sara talked her through it. "All right, now time me!" she shouted to Sara as she got Sunny in position.

Sara gave her the signal and Sunny leaped forward.

"I don't understand. It's impossible." Sara's eyes were fixed on the slim figure that raced around the barrels. "Nobody learns barrel racing that fast." Alison came flying around the third barrel and raced toward them, bent low over the saddle.

"Whew! That was a blast!" she shouted, pulling Sunny to a halt in front of them. "How was my time?"

Sara looked up from her stopwatch. "Twenty-one seconds. Incredible."

"I can go a lot faster than that. I was holding Sunny back the whole time." She leaned down and patted his sweaty neck. "You love this, don't you, big boy?"

Sara shook her head. "He's out of condition. Walk him around and let him cool off before you race again." She tilted her head to one side. "Alison, have you been fooling us? Have you run barrels before?"

"Of course not, I'm a city girl." Alison was still panting,

exhilarated from her ride. "Becky will tell you."

Becky nodded. "She's never done it before." Trust Alison to be so good at everything, she thought, frowning.

"Well, she rides like a pro. It's great for Sunny to be getting his legs back." Sara was glowing like a proud mother.

"He'd like to go again, I can tell," Alison said. The big palomino was fidgeting like a rock star ready to go on stage.

"Don't rush him." Sara was firm. "Just lope him nice and steady around the ring. Rob, maybe you should get rid of the barrels so he doesn't think he's going to race."

"I'll help!" Becky cried. She didn't want Rob lifting the big barrels.

He gave her a puzzled look. "Okay, if you want to."

Becky squirmed. He thinks I'm being pushy, she thought. I don't want him to suspect I know about his condition. But she followed Rob to the end of the ring and helped him hoist an empty steel barrel to one side.

"Can you ride like your cousin?" Rob asked as they walked to the second barrel. Alison was loping Sunny around the ring, sitting straight and relaxed on the horse's back.

"No, not like her." Becky thought of all the hours she'd spent in the saddle. "I never rode for fun, or in a competition. Riding's always been work for me. Rounding up stray calves, stuff like that."

"That's right. You're *not* a city girl." Rob grinned, and Becky felt her face getting hot. Was that good? That she wasn't from the city?

"Tell me more about this Mustang Mountain Ranch your folks have," Rob said. He rolled the second barrel to the edge of the ring while Becky hovered anxiously around him.

"It doesn't really belong to my parents. It's a government ranch—Rob! Look out!" Becky yanked his arm, pulling him out of Sunny's path.

"What's the matter?" He stared at her.

"I thought Sunny might …"

"Sunny would never ride over me." Rob shook his head. "You sure are jumpy this morning. What's wrong? Want to tell me about it?"

"No, I mean, there's nothing wrong … with me." Becky blushed, knowing she was getting herself in deeper.

"Alison? You're jealous because your cousin's suddenly so good at riding barrels, is that it?"

Becky thought she'd better grab at that convenient explanation. It was better than the truth. "I guess so," she mumbled.

"Well, don't worry. It's not such a big deal." Rob had grabbed the third barrel and rolled it out of the way. They rejoined Sara, who was making notes on a clipboard.

"I'm going to set up a training schedule for them." Sara still wore a look of stunned surprise. "That girl's *good!* Don't you think, Rob?"

"The clock doesn't lie," Rob agreed.

"I think she should enter the next amateur event," Sara said. "I think she could win."

"Probably could." Rob nodded. "Hey, Sara, Becky and

I are going to do some work with Shadow. If you can tear yourself away from the *stars* here, you might take a look at how we're doing."

"Sure," Sara said, but Becky knew she wasn't listening. Her eyes and attention were all on Alison and her palomino gelding.

"She won't come," Rob muttered as they headed for the barn. He held the barn door open for Becky and she thought she saw a twist of pain in his eyes. She felt a pang for him—how much did his illness hurt? He was only sixteen years old and he was so brave, without his parents and facing this disease. She loved the way he stood back to let her go through the barn door first— good manners obviously came naturally to him. Becky ached with joy and pity and fear for Rob all at once. She couldn't let him ride Shadow!

CHAPTER 13

HORSE GENTLING

"Horse trainers used to break a horse by tying her down in the hot sun," Rob said. They were looking at Shadow over the door of her stall a few minutes later. "They believed that you had to break a horse's spirit before you could teach it anything. But I prefer the term 'starting a horse.' It's gentler."

Shadow looked a little less dangerous, Becky thought. Being out in the pasture had done her good. She didn't flatten her ears when you approached. But she still had hard, tight eyes that looked at you with a mixture of fear and distrust.

"It's time she got used to a saddle and a rider on her back again," Rob said.

Becky threw him a startled glance. "Today?" Cousin

Terri-Lyn had started Shadow last October, but no one had ridden her since then.

She gathered her courage to tell a huge lie. She was still scared of Shadow, but now she was more scared of Rob riding her. "I thought I'd like to start riding Shadow myself, if that's okay with you."

Rob's eyebrows rose. "I got the impression you weren't into horses that much."

Under the gaze of his glacier blue eyes, Becky was forced to tell part of the truth. "Well, I'm not. But I was there when Alison adopted Shadow in Wyoming. The poor little thing was so miserable, being captured and taken away from her free life. She almost died. I feel responsible for her. I want to make sure all that pain and trouble wasn't for nothing."

"Sure," Rob said slowly. "But this horse doesn't need any more pain and trouble. Are you sure you can handle her? You can't quit in the middle."

Becky gulped. "I'd like to try."

"She'll know if you're afraid," Rob said gently. "She has to trust that you know what you're doing, that it's okay to have a rider on her back."

Becky could feel her cheeks getting red. She *was* afraid and she *didn't* know what she was doing.

Rob looked doubtful. "I'm willing to take her on, you know."

Becky held her ground. "There's another reason." She was prepared for Rob's resistance. "I have a filly at home named Breezy. She's the only horse I've ever really liked.

I helped with her foaling, at night, in the middle of the wilderness at Mustang Mountain."

"That must have been exciting," Rob said.

"Too exciting." Becky remembered the moonlit ride back to the ranch with Breezy draped over the saddle in front of her. "There were wolves and a cougar out that night."

"Hey, this Mustang Mountain Ranch sounds interesting." Rob's face lit up.

"It gets pretty wild up there," Becky sighed. "But the thing is, Breezy won't be a helpless little foal when I get home. She'll be a big strong yearling. I want to be able to train her, without being ... scared."

Rob stared at her. "So you *are* afraid of horses!"

"Yeah ..." Becky blew out a big breath of air. "I never know what horses are going to do. I'm afraid they'll hurt me—throw me off, or kick me, or step on me. I've been like that since I got thrown from a horse when I was little."

"And you think training a half-wild mustang is going to help that?" Rob looked even more doubtful.

"I hope so." Becky stuck her hand in her pocket and brought out a small carrot. She held it out flat on her palm. Shadow took a few cautious steps toward her. Then she lowered her head and gobbled the outstretched carrot.

Becky offered her another. "I think Shadow is like me," she said. "She doesn't trust people the way I don't trust horses. We have to learn together. I'll get started next week."

"I don't know," Rob said. "It sounds a bit crazy."

Shadow was munching her carrot. Her whole body language had relaxed. It *is* crazy, Becky wanted to shout. But if it's the only way I can stop *you* from getting hurt, I'm going to do it. She guessed this must be love—caring so much about Rob that she stopped worrying about what was going to happen when she actually had to get on Shadow's back.

✱

"See? I told you I could do it!" Alison was dancing with glee on the walk to the bus stop. "Sara thinks I could be a champion barrel racer if I wanted."

Becky scuffed her toes in the loose gravel. "I thought all you wanted was to get back to your super-cool life in New York."

Alison stopped dancing. "Maybe I do, maybe I don't. What are you so touchy about? Are you mad because I'm so good at barrel racing?"

"No, I'm used to you being Ms. Hot-Shot! Ever since I've known you you've been bragging about something or other."

"Touchy, touchy, touchy," Alison teased. "What's the matter? You and Rob having problems?"

Becky thought she might explode. How was she going to stand living with Alison until school ended in June? "I won't fight with you, I won't fight with you, I won't fight with you," she muttered over and over between clenched teeth.

When she had control of herself, she said, "No. Rob

and I had a great time. I'm going to start training Shadow next week."

Alison gave her a puzzled look. "I thought you said Rob was going to do the training."

"I changed my mind." Becky tried to sound casual. "I think I'd like to give horse-gentling a try."

"Go ahead," Alison said breezily. "I have much more exciting things to do." She took a few running steps and jumped in the air. "Sara's going to enter me in the Spring Challenge in May."

That night, as soon as Alison was in the bathroom, Becky rushed to the computer to e-mail Meg:

Alison is now a barrel racer, actually entered in a race. It's weird. But I can hardly think about her anymore. I'm so worried about Rob, even though he seems okay. Can you see what else you can find out about this disease? At least I've convinced him to let me work with Shadow. But I'm scared. I need help. How did you start training Patch? If I'm going to ride Shadow, where do I begin?

Meg quickly sent back a message.

Patch was never as wild as Shadow, so it was easier. But, she does spook more easily than other horses I've ridden, and then she's likely to scoot. I've taken some rough falls! I think it's just because she's a "wild horse," and in the wild, she had to be ready to run. I never know what's going to frighten her—a piece of paper, a flap of canvas, even a rock. The one thing she's totally terrified of is plastic bags!

Shadow will probably be the same. You have to convince her that she can trust you. You're her leader and she'll be safe if she follows you. Last summer, Thomas told me to think like a horse, but sometimes that's not so easy to do. Try to remember that Shadow doesn't want to hurt you, and as she trusts you more, she'll spook less, or at least not bolt when she does.

Speaking of Thomas, he still hasn't e-mailed. I'm going to e-mail him one more time. Wish me luck!

love,
Meg

CHAPTER 14

MAKING FRIENDS

For the next two weeks, Alison took lessons from Sara almost every day. After every lesson, she boasted about a faster time, a new accomplishment on Sunny.

Becky spent her after-school and weekend hours with Shadow. Rob hovered like a mother hen, wanting her to get on with riding her, but Becky remembered Meg's message about trust and was determined not to rush the mustang. If she was going to ride Shadow, *she* was going to have to earn her trust.

At first, Becky just sat patiently outside Shadow's stall, watching her sleep, or munch hay, or hang out with Chompster. She brought bags of carrots and fed them both a steady stream of treats. Chompster was soon her fast friend. The grumpy little mule would lift his head and bray when he heard her footsteps in the barn.

Slowly, Shadow began to look for Becky, too. She'd be there, at the stall door, poking her head out for a carrot, or she'd come to the fence on sunny days, when Rob had put her in the pasture. On those days, Becky sat on an old water trough and watched Shadow. She liked to run to the far fence and just stand there, head pointed toward the mountains, sniffing the breeze.

"I wonder if she smells the open range," Becky said to Rob one day. "I wonder if she'll ever forget and be happy inside fences and barns."

"She needs something to occupy her," Rob said. "I thought you were going to get a saddle and bridle on her."

"Don't rush us," Becky said, shrugging her shoulders. "We're not ready yet."

But the day came, in mid-April, when she knew it was time. She had got up from her seat at the trough and was walking back to the barn when she felt a nudge on her shoulder—Shadow's nose. The paint mare was following her. Without thinking about it, Becky threw her arm around Shadow's neck and reached in her pocket for a carrot. "Friends?" she whispered. Shadow bobbed her head and nuzzled her ear.

Becky went racing to the arena to tell Rob and the others her good news.

When she got there, Alison was loping Sunny around the ring, her face beaming with pride. Sara was hopping up and down on one leg shouting, "She broke seventeen seconds! She's ready for the Spring Challenge!"

Even Rob was clapping and cheering.

After that, Becky's news didn't seem so earth-shattering.

That night, Meg sent an e-mail to Becky:

Hey, you'll never believe this! I finally heard from Thomas. He moved and then had computer problems, and by the time he got hooked up, he'd lost my e-mail address. I was so happy to hear from him—but I guess you figured that out!

And that's not all! He says he's going to be at the Calgary Stampede in July, as part of Indian Village, and he's going to bring Wildfire. I've got to get there, somehow. I've just got to see him again!

lots of love,
Meg

Meg and Thomas had finally connected! Meg might come to the Stampede in July! A big grin spread across Becky's face. She shouted for Alison. "Come see this e-mail from Meg."

"Wow!" Alison said, peering over her shoulder. "So Thomas has come back into the picture." She shrugged. "I guess you never know with men."

"It was just a lost address," Becky marveled. "I always thought Thomas and Meg had something special. And look! He's trained Wildfire so well he can bring him to the Stampede." Wildfire was a fiery red wild stallion from the Rockies. Thomas had captured him and taken him home to be the foundation stallion of his herd of mountain trail horses.

"I wonder if Meg will actually make it out here to see Thomas," Alison mused. "That would be so romantic." Then her face lit up. "*And* they could both watch me race. Wouldn't that be great?"

"You're not riding at the Calgary Stampede!" Becky cried.

"Well, not this year. But maybe next year." Alison tilted up her chin defiantly.

Becky sat gaping at her. Alison riding in the biggest rodeo of them all? Two months ago, that would have seemed as likely as a trip to Jupiter!

"Move over." Alison nudged her out of the desk chair. "I want to tell Meg about the Spring Challenge."

CHAPTER 15

SURVIVAL INSTINCTS

A week later, on a quiet Sunday morning, Becky finally felt ready to get on Shadow's back. After that wonderful day when Shadow had nudged her shoulder, Becky had reintroduced her to the bridle and reins, the saddle blanket and saddle—all the things she would need to be ridden. And she'd come to know many things about Shadow, not just as a horse, or even a wild horse, but as an individual with a definite personality.

First, the little mare hated to be approached head-on, especially with anything new. You had to come up slowly on her left side and pretend you had no special interest in her.

You also had to talk to her—not in a loud voice, but constantly. She liked to hear that she was a smart horse, a clever horse, not easily fooled, and that you knew better than to try to put one over on her. Her ears twitched forward, and her eyes softened whenever Becky talked to her.

Becky found that comforting Shadow comforted her, too. She could feel Shadow twitch nervously as she settled the thick wool saddle blanket into position. "It's okay," she soothed. "Just the same old blanket you've been sniffing and nibbling all week. Nothing scary."

She turned and picked up the light saddle she and Rob had selected for Shadow.

It had taken patience and countless tries before the mare accepted this weird weight on her back. Then more tries to do up the cinch around her belly. Still more to get her used to a bridle again. But now, after a week of training, the moment had come.

"All right," Becky sighed. "It's now or never, little horse."

She led Shadow, saddled and bridled, out of the barn into the round pen. The sudden light made them both blink.

"Steady," Becky said, trying to still the butterflies in her own stomach.

A figure appeared, silhouetted against the sun.

"What's up?" It was Rob.

"You'll be happy to hear I'm finally going to ride Shadow." Becky flushed. "But we don't need an audience."

"I'd be glad to get on her," Rob said. He walked toward Becky, and she could see his pale face shaded by the hat brim.

Sometimes Becky forgot that Rob was sick, he seemed so normal. But then he'd look especially pale one day or would disappear for a doctor's visit, and she'd remember. During one of those visits, Becky came across a rack of his old ribbons and trophies in the back of the barn. Rob had been a champion rider, too! Of course, he would have had to give that up when he was diagnosed.

Another time, she interrupted him gulping down pills in the tack room. And once, when he bent to lift a bale of hay, she glimpsed a stainless steel chain around his neck. He must wear one of those medical tags that gives your condition in case of an emergency. Poor Rob! He was too young.

She looked up into his blue eyes. "No, I've come this far. Shadow's used to me." The thought of getting thrown was frightening, but the thought of Rob flying through the air and thudding into the hard-packed dirt was worse.

"Stand back," she told Rob. "I'm going to do this."

Becky had once seen a cowboy bucked off a green horse. One second he was in the saddle, the next he was in the dirt. There seemed to be no time in between. The horse had flicked the rider off his back as if he were an annoying fly.

She tried to wipe out that image as she approached Shadow's side.

"I'm not afraid of *her*," she told herself. "I'm afraid of something in my imagination. It's not real." Shadow was an intelligent horse, not some brainless bronc. She'd been so crushed by her capture from the wild and her separation from Patch that she had almost chosen death. Now Becky was her leader and the one she depended on for comfort and guidance. Shadow wouldn't hurt her. She was sure—well, almost sure—of that.

She wished Rob wasn't watching. It broke her concentration.

"Rob, can you get me Shadow's other bridle?" she asked. "I think she likes it better than this one."

"I think you're stalling." Rob grinned, but he turned on his heel and went to get the bridle.

"Okay, Shadow, we have to do this fast." Becky put her left foot in the stirrup, lifted herself straight up and threw her right leg over Shadow's back. Softly, lightly, she let herself down in the saddle, picked up the reins and gave Shadow a gentle nudge with her legs. "Let's go," she said in a matter-of-fact voice.

Shadow looked back over her shoulder as if to say, "Well, there you are, then," and walked toward the fence.

Becky glanced up and saw Rob come out of the barn and stand very still, watching them.

His face was tense, pleased and surprised all at the same time. "Look at you," he said. "Like Shadow knew all along what to do."

At that exact moment, a magpie flew into the paddock straight at Shadow. Its black and white feathers were shockingly bright in the sun.

Shadow spooked sideways so quickly that Becky had no time to collect herself before she was in midair. She fell with a bone-jarring thump.

For one ghastly second, she saw her vision again, the flashing hooves and the bared teeth above her. Instead, Shadow was running, loping around the pen with a wild look in her eye and the reins trailing.

Rob went to catch her.

"Rob, don't!" Becky yelled, but it was too late. Rob intercepted Shadow, safely gathered in her reins and brought her to a halt.

Becky picked herself up, shaking. She wasn't hurt, but she wanted to run, like Shadow, away from the frightening experience—the nightmare almost come true.

"The best thing is to get right back on her as if nothing happened," Rob called to her. "That was just a freak—I've never seen a magpie fly at a horse that way."

"I don't ... I can't," Becky struggled to speak.

"It's all right." Rob turned to Shadow. "I'll ride her."

"NO!" Becky shouted, running forward. "No, I'll do it. You're right—it's better if I get on her right away. I don't want her to think I'm scared."

"Are you sure?" Rob shook his head. "You look scared to me."

Becky took a deep breath and brushed back her hair. "That's just because I got the wind knocked out of me. I'll be okay. We'll be okay."

She wasn't having Rob get on Shadow, especially if the horse was going to throw riders that way. She took Shadow's reins from him, put them around Shadow's neck and stuck her foot in the stirrup again. "There's no problem," she whispered. "You had a scare, but everything's all right now. We're going to take a nice quiet walk around this pen, like we planned."

Back in the saddle, her heart in her mouth, Becky urged Shadow forward. She could feel the tension in the horse's body, like a wound-up spring. With every bit of energy, she fought back her own terror and told Shadow she would be fine, safe, nothing to worry about. Becky focused her energy on where she wanted Shadow to go and willed the horse to go there. When they had made three quiet circles of the pen, she gently pulled Shadow to a halt and slid from the saddle.

For a moment, Becky thought her legs wouldn't support her. But Rob was still watching, so she took a deep breath and forced herself to smile.

"Nice work." Rob walked over to them. "Looks like you might ride as well as Alison."

Becky let out her breath. He thinks that's what matters to me, she thought. Some kind of competition with Alison. Oh boy, if he only knew the truth!

"What's the matter? Why are you looking at me like that?" Rob asked.

"Sorry, it's nothing." Becky led Shadow toward the barn. She could tell Rob was still looking at her with a puzzled frown. There was so much she couldn't say!

That night, Becky sent the news to Meg:

I did it! I rode Shadow! I even got back on after she threw me. She didn't mean to toss me off—she spooked at a bird. And she moved away so she wouldn't hurt me. When I got back in the saddle, she was okay, a bit tense, but she trusted me enough to let me back on and walk around!

Rob wanted to ride Shadow, but I wouldn't let him. She's still unpredictable. I guess that's natural. Like you say, her survival instincts are stronger than most horses'. I can't take a chance on Rob getting thrown off the way I was. It happened so fast—there was no warning!

On the subject of Rob—have you found out anything more about this thrombo thing? I'm afraid to search the Web even in school, in case Alison catches on. Let me know what you find out about treatment, or cures, or what's dangerous.

Meg e-mailed back:

Way to go, Shadow! And way to go, Becky! I know how hard it must have been for you to get back on.

I searched some more about Rob's disease, but there's not much. It seems like they don't know the exact cause. Sometimes kids get it after a virus. And sometimes it just goes away by itself. Let's hope that's what happens in Rob's case. This must be so awful for you! I just want to give you a big hug—it's horrible being so far away.

I'm still working on getting to the Stampede. I'm teaching Alison's riding students, and I'm saving every cent for my ticket. Keep your fingers crossed.

got to go—love you,
Meg

CHAPTER 16

SPRING CHALLENGES

The Spring Challenge on May 7 was the first outdoor barrel race of the season. Pickups with large horse trailers rolled into the fairgrounds near Cochrane early Friday evening. The Twin Rocks trailer had bunks for Sara and Rob at the front and room for two horses and their gear in the back. Alison and Becky brought sleeping bags and a tent to pitch beside the trailer.

That night, there was a big barbecue and bonfire, with all the barrel racers and their families sharing steaks and sausages, baked potatoes and salad. Rob was one of the chefs, turning meat on a big outdoor grill.

"He looks pretty good in the firelight," Alison said. "It brightens him up a bit—he doesn't look so pale."

"Hmmm." Becky didn't want to talk about Rob. She

just wanted to watch him, talking and laughing, with the orange flames lighting up his face. The line of trailers, each with horses tied to them, stood out against the huge star-studded western sky.

Later, they stood and filled their plates with hot meat and crisp potatoes. "I notice you're not a vegetarian anymore." Becky pointed to the large steak sandwich on Alison's plate.

"Nope. That was just something my parents did to be trendy." Alison shrugged. "Anyway, how could you live out here and not eat meat?" She moved off to sit near Sara.

Rob came over with his own heaping plate and sat beside Becky on a bale of straw.

"What's the matter, isn't my cooking any good?" he asked. "You're hardly eating anything."

"No, it's delicious!" Becky was so filled with happiness at sitting next to Rob in the flickering firelight that there seemed to be no room in her for food.

"Do you think Alison's nervous about the race tomorrow?" Rob wondered.

Did they have to talk about Alison? "I don't think so," Becky answered. "She's convinced she's going to win."

"That's a tall order." Rob shook his head. "Lots of good riders here, and she's a beginner."

"How's Diane, the girl who fell?" Becky tried to change the subject.

"Better, but still not riding. She had a pretty bad concussion. And Dark Diamond had to be put down."

Becky felt a chill. Falling, hitting your head hard

enough to get a concussion—she didn't want to think about those things these days. She'd been riding Shadow steadily for the past two weeks, but she couldn't completely shake her fear that Shadow might bolt at any second and throw her to the ground.

"Are you worried about Alison?" Rob asked sympathetically.

Alison *again*. Becky shrugged and gave up. So much for a romantic conversation. "Not too much," she said.

Alison shocked everyone by placing second the next day. Becky heard the buzz going around the horse trailers. Who was the dark-haired girl riding Sunny?

Melissa Dale, the eleven-year-old phenom, came first, beating Alison by half a second.

"I ought to be able to beat a little kid like her," Alison fumed. "What makes her so good?" She was walking Sunny around the practice ring, cooling him off after his run. Becky and Sara were with her.

"Watch Melissa ride," Sara advised. "She rides Samarkand as if she never knew a second's fear or hesitation. She's focused—she knows where she wants to go. Did you see how straight her line was from the third barrel to the finish? Not a step wasted. That's because she hits the turn at just the right angle. Not too tight, not too wide."

"It's mostly the horse," Alison grumbled. She was tired of hearing about the marvelous Melissa.

"If you have that attitude, you'll never be a champion."

Sara gave her a disappointed glance from her clear blue eyes. "You don't have to win every time, but you do have to learn from your mistakes and recognize superior skill when you see it."

"Superior? That squirt?" Alison curled her lip. "Wait until next time. Sunny can outrun Samarkand any day, and I'll prove it." She patted Sunny's sweaty neck.

Sara ran loving eyes over the tall palomino. "He does look great, doesn't he? I think Sunny is at the top of his form. I can't wait to ride him again."

She looked at Alison and smiled. "I'm thinking that if you keep him in good condition, there's a chance, just a chance, that I might do some serious barrel racing this season after all. My leg's feeling a lot better."

Becky couldn't resist. "Wouldn't that be wonderful, Alison?" she asked innocently. She could almost hear her cousin grinding her teeth, and the look she shot Becky should have shriveled her into dust.

"I won't give up Sunny. I won't, and that's final. I want to ride him. I was the one who got him ready, and now Sara wants to waltz in and just take him back? No way!"

Alison was pacing their bedroom at home later that night.

"Alison, he's Sara's horse!" Becky was on her bed, arms around a large pillow.

"So? What horse am I going to barrel race if she takes Sunny away from me?"

Becky had an urge to throw her pillow at her cousin's pouty face. "You should be happy Sara's getting better," she pointed out.

"Well, I'm not. Why can't she just sit this season out, like she said she would?"

"You are so unbelievably selfish!" Becky finally did hurl the pillow at Alison.

"I don't know what you're talking about." Alison tossed the pillow back and whirled to study her reflection in the mirror. "I'm thinking of letting my hair grow—maybe as long as Meg's, or even Sara's." She held up a silk scarf to see the effect of long hair tied back.

She went on, "And I'm thinking of getting one of those shirts, you know ..."

"With the pearl buttons and the fringe?" Becky was being sarcastic, but Alison was too absorbed in her vision of herself as a cowgirl to notice.

"You know the ones?" she said. "Kind of fitted, and some Wrangler jeans, and maybe a belt with a ..."

"Big silver buckle?" Becky snorted. "Alison, you're kidding."

"Why? It would look great on me." Alison encircled her slim waist with her hands. "I want to look good up there on Sunny."

Becky pulled the pillow over her head, laughing. After all the times Alison had made fun of western dress! What a fake!

CHAPTER 17

She's My Horse

Sara started riding Sunny again the next week.

Alison stayed away from the riding ring when Sara and Sunny were practicing. Instead, she hung around Becky and Shadow, offering a steady critique of everything Becky was doing.

By this time, Becky had been riding Shadow for more than a month, first walking, getting her used to leg and rein commands. Shadow's Wyoming training had come back once she was comfortable with Becky in the saddle. She'd jogged and loped her in the ring for short periods, and Shadow was getting the hang of it.

"Look," Becky finally said one afternoon near the end of May, when Alison criticized the way she was brushing Shadow, "*I'm* training Shadow, not you. So butt out."

"Rob says she loves to run and she'd make a good barrel racing horse." Alison stood, hands on hips, while Becky unclipped Shadow from the crossties.

"So? I'm not going to barrel race her." Becky started to lead Shadow back to her stall.

"She's my horse," Alison said.

Becky turned and stared at her cousin. "Now you want *Shadow?*" she burst out. "Now that I'm riding her, and now that Sara is riding Sunny again? Where were you when Shadow was lonely and miserable?"

"I was a brat," Alison admitted. "I blamed her for everything that was wrong in my stupid life. But you're training her, and look how well she's doing. Why won't you let me try taking her around a few barrels—just to see how she does?"

Becky had the horrible feeling that Alison, as usual, was going to get her way in the end. But not before she put up a fight for Shadow.

"It's too soon," she insisted. "She's just getting used to the idea of being ridden. I wish I could get her up to Mustang Mountain this summer, where I could take her out on the trails, or ride her up the meadow." She gave Shadow a loving pat. "Maybe it's too soon for that, too, but she needs to know that she can have fun being ridden."

"Racing is fun," Alison shot back. "Can't you see how much Sunny likes it?"

"But Sunny is a trained barrel horse!" Becky felt her temper rising but fought it back. She must not fight with Alison in front of Shadow. She straightened her shoulders.

"Shadow was wild until last fall. You can't expect her to take to running barrels in front of a noisy crowd."

"Who said anything about a crowd? I just want to try her around a few barrels in the arena—slowly." Alison's dark eyes were steady and stubborn. "She's *my* horse, and I want her back."

Becky gulped. "Here, take her then." She handed Alison the lead rope, turned and stalked out of the barn before she exploded. This was so unfair. And so like Alison! When she wanted something, she pulled out all her ammunition and fired away. She didn't care who got hurt.

A few minutes later, she stood at the edge of the arena and watched Alison jog Shadow around the barrels.

It was a cool, late May evening and the sun's long slanted rays gleamed through the open doors. Becky's eyes were dazzled, but she could see Shadow going around the barrels. The sun turned her dark patches rosy brown. Becky caught her breath as Shadow loped home.

Alison was right. She looked born to barrel race.

Becky turned and blundered out of the ring, only to collide with Rob.

"Hey, what's this?" He held her at arm's length. "What's the matter? You look like you're about to self-destruct."

The setting sun lit Rob's face, too, seemed to shine through the thin flesh of his ears and cheeks. Becky choked back her feelings. "Nothing. Alison's training Shadow on the barrels."

"That's amazing." Rob glanced over her shoulder at

Alison and Shadow. "You've brought her along so well." He looked down at Becky's flushed face. "And you think it should be you in there, after all your work starting her. I agree." Rob shook his head. "It's that bossy cousin thing again, right?"

"Not just that," Becky turned back and watched Alison begin running the pattern again. "Shadow needs more time learning the fundamentals before she's run around barrels. I know her, and she needs to take things slow."

"Maybe," Rob said, "but she sure seems to be learning fast." Shadow was already leaning her compact, sturdy body into the turn as they loped around the second barrel. "Some horses are naturals."

Sara came up behind them. "And Alison is a natural rider. Look at her on that horse!" The tall blonde girl's eyes were alive with admiration. "Wow, she's good."

Becky almost wished a bird would fly into Alison's face. Anything to wipe off that smug look of victory as they came loping down the ring toward an imaginary finish line.

✳

That night, Becky had a call. It was her mom, at Mustang Mountain Ranch. Becky danced impatiently while her Aunt Marion talked to her sister, then handed her the phone.

"Hi, Becky." Her mom's voice was so warm and familiar Becky could almost smell the pines and high fresh mountain air.

"I was just tellin' Marion that the trails are finally open. Your dad and I would be down to see you, but we're a couple of hands short. We'll get there as soon as we can. Marion says there's room for us to stay."

"Sure," Becky said. "How's Dad?"

"Same as ever. Busy. Lots of foals coming this spring."

"How's Breezy?"

Her mom laughed. "You should see her! She's a beautiful deep red, like her sire, Wildfire. Going to be tall. As frisky a filly as I've ever seen. Be prepared for a big change in your little foal."

"I am. I'm glad." Becky thought with relief that she might not be afraid of Breezy's rambunctious frisking now. Working with Shadow had helped.

"How's school?" her mother wanted to know.

"Fine."

"And that stable where you and Alison are hangin' out? How's Alison's little mustang?"

"She's okay."

"Becky—what's wrong?" Her mother's voice sounded crackly with the bad connection.

"The signal's breaking up," Becky said.

"I'm not talking about the telephone. What's wrong with *you?*"

Becky longed to pour out her heart to her mother. But Aunt Marion and Alison were listening, and anyway, there was too much to tell. "I can't wait to see you!" she shouted into the phone.

"I get it, you can't talk now. Well, hang in there, honey. Whatever it is, I know you can straighten it out. And we'll have a good talk when we get there. Don't worry."

"I won't." The conversation was now more crackle than words. "Bye, Mom!"

She put the phone down and sat with a thump at the table, not wanting to look at her cousin or her aunt.

Aunt Marion cleared her throat. "I've had a call tonight, too," she said. "From Roger."

"Dad?" Alison raised an eyebrow. "What did he want?"

Becky got up to leave the kitchen. She really didn't want to be part of this conversation.

"You'd better stay." Her aunt put a hand on her shoulder. Becky could feel it shaking. "This might concern you."

"What!" Now both of Alison's eyebrows shot up in alarm. "I know. Dad wants you back. Well, I hope you told him …" She was looking at her mother's face. "Oh, no! You aren't thinking of going back!" Alison rose from the table. "Mother? Tell me."

"My job—" Marion Chant swallowed, "—hasn't turned out the way I'd hoped. And expenses are higher than I expected."

"Mother, you wouldn't go back for the money?" Alison looked truly horrified.

"It's not just that. I … well, we've been married a long time."

"*Were* married, you mean. Now you're separated. Soon you'll be divorced."

Becky almost felt sorry for her Aunt Marion. She knew how it felt to be on the receiving end of Alison's stubborn anger. "I think we might try again—" Her aunt faltered. "Wouldn't you like to go home? To New York?"

"Not *now*," Alison raged. "Now that I've found something I really love to do, and I'm good at. And the kids at school are finally starting to appreciate me."

It was true, Becky realized. Ever since the Spring Challenge and the change in Alison's wardrobe to western gear, she was a hit at school.

"I'm not having my life torn apart again!" Alison was pacing up and down the small kitchen. "What are you trying to do, Mother, put me into therapy?"

Becky had to put her head down on the table. A burst of laughter had almost escaped, and she knew her face would give her away. Alison was always the drama queen. Poor Aunt Marion! It wasn't funny. It wasn't a bit funny, she realized.

That night, Alison e-mailed Meg:

Meg, I know I haven't written lately, but I've been thinking about you, promise! I'm glad to hear that Thomas got in touch with you, and I hope you make it to the Stampede.

I'm starting to like it better out here, and wouldn't you know? Tonight Mom announces she's thinking of going back to New York and my dad. She'd better not! I don't want to leave right now. I don't know if Becky told you, but I'm training Shadow to barrel race. Becky thinks it's too soon, but Shadow's fantastic!

love,
your old buddy,
Alison

Meg answered:

Since you left, I've been teaching your riding students, and they took up a collection to help me get to the Stampede. Isn't that cool? I got a cheap ticket to Calgary near the end of Stampede week, but at least I'll make it for the final day. And Becky has invited me to Mustang Mountain for a couple of weeks after, which will be amazing. Good luck with the barrel racing, and try to be nice to Becky. She's worked hard starting Shadow, and she'll miss her if you're racing her.

more later,
Meg

Alison shot back:

Be nice to Becky? She didn't ask *me* to Mustang Mountain! Not that I care, because I'll be barrel racing on Sunny and Shadow, but she could have asked! Sara is going to let me ride Sunny in some events, even though her knee is getting better. You should see him run. I'm going to win lots of races on that horse!

be good!
Alison

CHAPTER 18

RODEO GIRL

Alison didn't waste time getting Shadow into a barrel racing competition.

"Couldn't she start this summer—I mean just in fun meets, nothing serious?" she asked Sara the next afternoon at Twin Rocks, where Becky and Alison found her doing knee-strengthening exercises in the tack room.

Sara raised her leg to the side and then swung it inward, holding on to a saddle rack. "I guess we could think about it. There's a mini rodeo this weekend at Harrison—they'll have barrel racing. Want to try Shadow there?"

"Sounds perfect." Alison beamed.

"Okay, I'll enter you." Sara stopped swinging her leg. "There. Fifty." She turned and smiled at Alison, her bright blue eyes happy. "I'm entering Sunny in some races this month, too."

"Do you want me to ride him?" Alison asked eagerly.

"No, you know, my knee's feeling so much stronger I think I'll try him myself."

"You don't want to rush it!" Alison tried to sound sincere. "I mean, the stress of competition could set you back …"

"I know it's a risk." A shadow crossed Sara's smooth forehead. "But if I want to go to vet college in the fall, I need money. I'm thinking I might still be able to race at the Stampede, but I've got to get at least one competition in before then." She turned to the saddle rack. "Maybe I'll just do another set of leg raises. See you later."

She called over her shoulder as Alison turned to go, "Warm up Shadow. I'll come time you in a few minutes."

Alison was fuming as she saddled Shadow. "Why can't she just wait a few more months? I was counting on riding Sunny in some more races this spring." She gave an impatient tug on Shadow's bridle. "I'll bet I'd win that race at the Harrison Rodeo on him."

Becky itched to grab the bridle out of Alison's uncaring hands. "Is that all you care about—winning?" she muttered. "How come when you were riding dressage you said you hated competition?"

Alison looked up, her dark eyes puzzled. "I did say that, didn't I? I guess it was because my mother was always nagging me to be as good as she was. But dressage wasn't my thing, it was hers."

"And this is your thing … barrel racing?" Becky felt the flush rise in her cheeks.

"Sure, why not?" Alison led Shadow toward the ring. "I'm obviously great at it. Come on, Shadow, if I'm going to ride you, you're going to have to get better, fast!"

✳

Harrison was a small ranching town farther into the foothills. From here, the Rockies seemed close enough to touch. But if the setting was awe-inspiring, Becky thought, the town itself looked tired and run down. Half the stores on the main street were closed, and the buildings at the fairgrounds were leaning.

Alison didn't seem to notice, as the Twin Rocks trailer pulled into the grassy field near the tumbledown grandstand. "Our first rodeo," she cried to Shadow as she led her out of the trailer. "You're going to love this."

Becky didn't think so. Shadow was already trying to back away from the country music that blared from the announcer's stand.

Alison tied Shadow to the trailer while she groomed and then saddled her. Then she warmed her up in the grassy area before riding her toward the contestants' gate.

As they got near the gate, Becky could see that people were lining up to pay admission. There would be the usual events: calf roping, team penning, steer wrestling, bareback and saddle bronc riding, as well as bull riding and barrel racing.

Becky had seen young cowboys practicing bull riding

in Wyoming. It was a crazy sport. Guys got hurt, sometimes killed. This was such a small-time rodeo, would the horses be safe? She'd heard of a bull killing a horse when it escaped from its chute. It had taken only seconds. Bulls were enormous and dangerous.

"I don't want to go in." Becky held up her hand. "I'll just wait in the truck."

Alison glared down at her. "What's the matter with you?"

"Nothing's wrong with me." Becky glared back. "I just don't want to watch Shadow being put through this."

"This what?"

"This barrel race. She's not a rodeo horse—she's a mustang. All this noise and flash—this tearing around barrels just so you can show off your new cowgirl image." Becky stopped, choked with words she wanted to say. You're a fake!

"You're just jealous," Alison hissed. "Go ahead. Stay over there and sulk. See if I care."

Becky watched her ride away, then turned her back on the bleachers and walked to the trailer. She sat in its open back and stared up at the mountains. They seemed so close, the snowy peaks etched in sunlight, the forested slopes dark green. Below them, spring grass covered the foothills like a carpet of soft green fleece.

An hour passed, then two. Cheers rose from the stands behind her, music blared and the announcer's speaker was a constant irritating growl.

And then Alison was standing in front of her, holding

a hot and lathered Shadow. The dark patches of her hide looked almost black with sweat.

"We made three runs," Alison crowed. "I made the finals! You can cool Shadow down while I get ready." She handed the reins to Becky, turned on her heel and marched away. Becky watched her join a clutch of admirers, mostly male.

Becky stroked Shadow's cheek. Her nostrils were still wide with the effort of running, and she looked longingly at the water bucket. Becky led her away from the trailer—she didn't want to give her too much water until she cooled off.

"Poor Shadow," Becky murmured.

Shadow bobbed her head and nuzzled Becky's shoulder. Suddenly she stopped and looked up at the mountains. She had that same stance Becky had seen when she stood at the pasture fence at Twin Rocks, gazing toward the foothills.

"I bet you'd like to be out there, wouldn't you?" Becky pressed her face against Shadow's hot cheek. "Out there where you could go for a good run, or stop and graze and not feel fences all around you. Like the hills in Wyoming."

All at once, Becky felt a powerful urge to get in Shadow's saddle and ride toward those mountains. She could hear Alison's sneering voice in her ear—"You're always so impulsive"—and she knew she shouldn't do it ... but how much trouble could they get into if she just rode the mare in the direction of the mountains? It was the ride she'd been dreaming about since she rode Shadow for the first time, and she might not get another chance.

Without listening to any more inner warnings, Becky swung up into the saddle. Shadow pricked up her ears as they started down the dirt road that led from the edge of town to the fairgrounds and beyond. Becky thought she could almost hear the horse saying, "Well, at last, we're going in the right direction."

"Not a long ride," she told Shadow. "We have to get you back before Alison wants you for the finals. As if you cared about that." She reached under Shadow's mane and patted her wet neck.

She kept Shadow at a relaxed pace, thrilling to the feel of being on her again, out in the open, wishing the ride could last forever. How totally unfair it was that she was Alison's horse—Alison who cared about nothing but showing off! The sounds of the rodeo faded as they rode away from town.

The rumble of a heavy truck somewhere behind them broke into Becky's thoughts. It couldn't be on this road, she thought, it's not wide enough for a big truck. The next instant, the transport was bearing down on them, and the blare of its horn seemed right on their heels.

Shadow panicked. They shot off the road just as the transport careened by in a cloud of dust and gravel.

For a moment, the dust blinded Becky. Shadow was running as if she'd never had a bit in her mouth, terrified, out of control. She raced through a gap in the roadside fence. In seconds, they were far from the road, tearing downhill. The ground flashed by and then Becky looked up and saw another fence.

Frantically, she screamed and tried to turn Shadow, but the mare was beyond listening, running with all the instinct of a prey animal to escape— running straight into three strands of barbed wire.

At the last second, Shadow veered from the fence, but it was too late. Becky was thrown in a long arc away from the deadly barbs.

But Shadow, she saw with horror as she struggled to her feet, was caught fast in the fence.

CHAPTER 19

IN THE FENCE

"Shadow!" Becky screamed. "Don't move!"

But poor Shadow was beyond listening to anything she had to say. A strand of the cruel wire was between her forelegs, another under her belly. Whichever way she moved, they tore at her flesh.

Becky felt as though the rips were to her own body. This was all her fault!

Shadow was neighing with terror and pain. Her eyes were red-rimmed with fear. Becky knew she was as dangerous now as she had been when she exploded in the stall. But this was not an unknown out-of-control horse. This was Shadow, who had trusted her, who she had betrayed into a ride that could cost her her life.

Becky struggled to get to Shadow's head and hold her.

The wire clutched at her and she felt searing pain down her forearm.

"Stop fighting," she gasped at Shadow. "Trust me one more time and just stop fighting. I'll get you free, I promise."

She had seen animals caught in fence wire before, on the ranches where she'd grown up. Sometimes they died if they struggled too much and help didn't come in time. A ranch horse knew pretty well to stay away from the deadly wire. But Shadow had never seen this kind of fence on the open range, and at Blue Barn and Twin Rocks, the fences were rails, designed to be safe for horses. Barbed wire was for cattle ranches with vast property. Cheap and practical. Fragile-looking, but dangerous.

Finally, Shadow stood still long enough for Becky to get close. She held the wire away from the little horse and tugged at it. It was taut as a guitar string. She needed wire cutters. "I'll get you out, somehow," she whispered fiercely. "I won't give up."

Now that Shadow was calmer, Becky could study the situation. Blood was dripping down Shadow's forelegs and belly, where the barbs pierced her hide, but as far as Becky could see, the wounds were not too deep, yet. If only she could keep Shadow quiet long enough to figure out how to free her.

She kicked at the nearest fence post. It was set firmly in the ground. Even the force of Shadow running into the fence hadn't loosened it. Sometimes the staples that held the wire to the post were old and rusty, but these were new. She yanked with all her strength. The wire cut into her hands, but the staples refused to budge.

"Steady, Shadow." Becky fought down her panic. "Easy, girl," she soothed, trying not to look at the blood. "We'll figure this out."

Something to cut the wire. But there was nothing, just open country in all directions, with the road leading back to the fairgrounds and town. No use shouting for help—nobody would hear her.

Nothing to do but wait until someone came down the road and hope they would see her. Nothing to do but stand by Shadow's head and try to keep her from struggling. Every move, however small, made the razor-sharp barbs cut deeper.

The sun had set over the mountains to the west, and the foothills were in deep shadow. A cold wind blew down from the slopes. Becky started to shiver. Shadow was shivering, too, from shock and pain.

"Please come." Becky stared at the road and begged. "Please, somebody come."

The rodeo grounds had its lights on now. She couldn't hear the music, but the garish lights looked like a Christmas tree from a distance. She hadn't realized she'd ridden that far.

I was an idiot, Becky thought. A total, complete stupid idiot. What was I thinking, riding Shadow away from the rodeo? Is Alison right? Am I just jealous? She clenched her teeth to stop the shivering. How could I have risked Shadow's life, and my own, like this? It was a familiar feeling, this being sorry too late. If I get out of this, Becky promised herself, I'll never do something so impulsive again.

In a few minutes, it would be too late for anyone to see her from the road. It would be dark.

CHAPTER 20

SOMEONE ON THE ROAD

Becky strained to see through the gathering dark. There were lights, coming down the road. A car? Whatever it was, it was moving very slowly.

"Help!" Becky hollered. "Help me over here!"

She kept shouting until she saw the lights leave the road. The vehicle bumped down the hill toward her. "Oh, Shadow," she sobbed, "someone's coming."

It was getting dark maddeningly fast. "I'm over here! My horse is in the fence. Come quick." Becky shouted until her throat hurt.

It was the Twin Rocks truck she realized, as it jolted closer. And it was Rob who opened the driver's side door and stepped out.

"What in blazes? Looks like you've got yourself in a

pretty bad mess." Rob shut the truck door quietly and walked slowly toward them so as not to frighten Shadow. "We've been looking everywhere for you. Sara and Alison are combing the streets in town."

"How did you know … I'd be out here?" Becky shivered with cold and relief.

"I didn't know, but I had an idea you might take off for the wide open spaces." Rob was looking at Shadow, examining the cuts as well as he could. Becky could tell he was furious. "What were you thinking of—never mind!" He reached toward the wire.

"Rob, no!"

"What's the matter?"

"You shouldn't be near this sharp wire. You might get cut." All Becky could think of was Rob's illness. His blood didn't clot properly. If he cut himself, he could hemorrhage.

"So what? You've got a few snags yourself, by the look of you. We've got to get Shadow out of here." Rob had come up close and was staring down at Becky. "We need to cut this wire. I'll go back to the trailer for tools. You'll have to stay here."

He took off his jacket and wrapped it around her. "Try to keep Shadow from struggling and making things worse. Can you hold out till I get back?"

She wasn't sure she could, but Becky nodded. "I'm sorry," she said in a low voice.

"You do have some things to be sorry about. Worry about them later. I'll hurry back as fast as I can."

Becky watched Rob climb into the truck and bump up the hill toward the road. How could she keep him from getting close to that wire when he got back?

*

Wrapped in darkness, Becky finally saw the pickup come toward her, its lights blazing. Alison and Sara jumped out and Rob followed them with a large toolbox. Becky winced when she saw Rob with a pair of sharp wire cutters, but she was helpless to protest. While Rob and Sara worked with the wire cutters to free Shadow, she had to endure the full force of Alison's anger.

"What?" Alison threw up her arms. "Would you rather Shadow died than barrel raced? Is that it? Or is it just that you couldn't stand to see me having fun?" Her voice ripped through Becky. "No, I know what it is. I was going to win that rodeo final, and you can't stand to see me doing well in something you're too chicken to even try! Do you know how it felt to have to scratch my name from the finals because I COULDN'T FIND MY HORSE?" Alison's voice rose to a shriek.

"Alison, stop. I'm sorry." Becky grabbed her arm. "Look, I did a stupid thing, but I'll never do it again. Shadow is your horse, and I won't interfere anymore."

"Well, I couldn't do her any more damage barrel racing than you did running her into a barbed-wire fence! Look at her. Poor thing!"

Becky couldn't stand to look. In the glare of the headlights, Rob was cutting the wire at the fence post and pulling it away from that end. He shouldn't be anywhere near that sharp wire! Becky thought frantically.

Sara was untangling Shadow. She was born to be a vet, that was sure. With a steady hand, she worked the wire away from Shadow's legs and underbelly and applied emergency treatment to stop the bleeding.

"Can one of you come and help hold her head?" Sara called. "She's getting anxious."

"You go." Becky shoved Alison forward.

"Chicken!"

"I'm not chicken, but she's your horse."

"And you got her into this mess. You get her out. And if you're not chicken, prove it by racing her around the barrels when she gets better!" Becky could hear the fury in her cousin's voice. "And then you'll be sorry you robbed her of winning her first rodeo!"

"Alison ... a little rodeo like that doesn't matter," Becky said.

"It mattered to me. It mattered to Shadow, too. She was running her heart out in there."

Sara interrupted them. "Stop arguing and get over here. Fast!"

Becky ran forward and stood near Shadow's face, tears running down her cheeks. Rob had turned the truck so Sara could see in the headlights' beams, and Shadow's cream patches stood out clearly. So did the rim of white around her frightened eyes. Becky cradled Shadow's head in her arms, saying soothing words, concentrating on making a connection through the fear and confusion in the horse's mind, calming Shadow's desperate need to run.

"That's right. Good. Almost done." Sara worked feverishly. "There. She's out of the wire, and I've stopped the bleeding. Now we've got to get her back to the road and into the trailer."

Sara wasn't looking at Becky. Becky could only imagine what she was thinking. The tall blonde girl who once seemed like she could be a friend, someone to look up to, now must hate her.

Sara got back into the truck, where Alison was already sitting, and banged the door shut. "I'll go ahead and get the trailer hooked up," she called to Rob. "Can you see well enough to lead Shadow to the road?"

"I've got a flashlight," he called back. "And Shadow can see in the dark just fine." He picked up Shadow's reins. "You coming?" he said to Becky.

"No, I'm going to sit out here and get eaten by coyotes." Becky handed him back his jacket. "I feel so stupid."

"You're shivering—keep the coat," Rob said.

*

That night, Alison poured her heart out to Meg, far away in New York.

What a crazy, mixed-up day today! First, I raced Shadow for the first time and we made the finals. I was so proud. Then, for some unknown reason, Becky took off on Shadow and rode her into a barbed-wire fence. I'm not kidding!

How could Becky hurt Shadow like that?! She says she loves her and then rides off on a strange road in the middle of a rodeo. Is she crazy? Shadow loves to race—I'm not forcing her to do this. Maybe if Becky rode Shadow in a real barrel race, she'd believe me!

Are you really coming to the Stampede next month? I hope so—there's so much I want to tell you. It's totally useless trying to talk to Becky!

My dad is still trying to convince Mom and me to move back. He's coming to the Stampede. Maybe when he gets away from Grandmother Chant, he'll actually transform into a human being.

I have so much else to tell you, but I've got to go. I'll let you know how Shadow's doing. I'd sure like to make Becky pay for what she did to Shadow. She says she's sorry, but she's not sorry enough!

love you, and miss you!
Alison

CHAPTER 21

GAME OVER

"Here I am again," Becky groaned two weeks later, "doing something Alison talked me into. I'm probably going to fall flat on my face!" Since the accident, Alison had been unbearably bossy. Becky had tried to make it up to her by doing extra dishes, finishing her math homework and lending her clothes whenever she asked. She'd spent hours with Shadow trying to regain her trust.

Now Becky was getting ready to do one last thing to make it up to Alison. She was going to ride Shadow around the barrels at Twin Rocks. She had healed fast, and the cuts from the barbed wire were just thin scabs on her dark chest, belly and legs.

"You're going to see how Shadow loves to barrel race, and then you'll say you're sorry for doubting me, and I'll know you really mean it!" Alison announced as Becky led Shadow into the arena. "I'll be watching." She marched away.

"I'm being set up, I can feel it," Becky said to Rob as she climbed into Shadow's saddle and got her feet set in the stirrups.

"Maybe." Rob nodded. He had been cool since the accident, and Becky knew he was still disappointed in her.

"But I don't have a choice. I have to do this," she sighed.

"Yep," Rob agreed.

"Okay ... GO!" Alison shouted from the other end of the ring.

Becky gave Shadow a nudge with her legs and leaned slightly forward.

Shadow took off as if jet-propelled. Before Becky had time to think, they were swinging around the first barrel, and she was clutching the saddle horn to stay on.

They whirled around the second barrel and headed for the third. Becky saw a flash of Alison's triumphant face. Then they were dashing back to Rob at the other end of the ring. Becky threw herself off Shadow's back.

"That was a pretty decent time." Rob was looking at the stopwatch in his hand.

"Shadow would make a good cow horse," Becky panted. "She's got good speed and turns quickly."

Alison came running up. "Get back up on her. You can't just jump off! She's got to cool down."

Becky obediently climbed onto Shadow. "Well?" Alison said. "What did you think? How did she feel?"

"Smooth and fast." Becky leaned forward to pat Shadow.

"I knew you'd like it. That's why I had Sara enter you and Shadow in the junior barrels at the next fun meet, here in Horner Creek."

"Aren't you riding Shadow?"

"Sara's going to let me ride Sunny at the fun meet." Alison's eyes appeared wide and innocent. "So it will be perfect. We'll both be racing. You have a week to practice."

Becky peered down at her. What was all this? Would Alison be satisfied once she rode Shadow in a barrel race?

✱

As soon as she saw the other entrants for the junior barrels at the Horner Creek fun meet, Becky understood how Alison had set her up.

"You're making me race against babies!" There was no one anywhere near Becky's age in the race.

Alison shrugged. "They start young. It's open to anyone under sixteen. That's you."

"I'm going to be so embarrassed." Becky stared at Alison.

"It's your first race." Alison shrugged again.

And my last, Becky vowed. This was so humiliating. There were a lot of kids from Horner Creek High in the crowd. She could see Jake Grady and the other older competitors sitting back in lawn chairs, smiling and laughing.

"The little kids are so cute." Alison smirked. "Don't you think?"

You planned this to make me look like a jerk, was what Becky was thinking, but she clenched her jaw tight. She would ride Shadow in this stupid race and then they would be even. No more payback.

Just then, Sara came up to them, leading Sunny. "Hey, Alison, Becky," she said. "Great day, isn't it?" She patted Shadow. "I entered you and Sunny in this event, too." She grinned at Alison. "I thought he could use the warm-up, and I'm too old for junior barrels."

Becky could see a tornado of emotions sweep over Alison's smooth features. "I thought I was riding Sunny in the last race," she choked.

"No, I decided to ride that race. My knee's feeling great today."

One of Alison's last chances to ride Sunny in a barrel race! And it was the junior race! Becky bit her lower lip to keep from grinning. Sometimes, revenge backfired.

Alison was sitting on Sunny's back, waiting for her turn. The last rider had knocked over the second barrel, and a man in a green shirt ran out to put it back in position. He smoothed the dirt around the barrel with his hand and ran to the sidelines.

"Oh, for pity's sake, let's get this over with," Alison muttered.

Becky was to ride right after Alison, and she circled Shadow in the start area to keep her warmed up.

The announcer came on the loudspeaker. "The next rider will be Becky Sandersen on Shadow."

Becky and Alison stared at each other. "They've mixed us up," Alison said crossly. "Oh, go ahead, it doesn't matter."

"Not to you, maybe," Becky said. "I'm not ready!"

But Alison was right, it wasn't worth making a fuss about. Becky gathered herself and started toward the gate. She could feel the eagerness in Shadow's body as she collected herself for their takeoff. "Easy now," Becky murmured. Once they crossed the electric eye beam, the clock would start, and she wanted Shadow to be in a decent position.

"Okay, go!" She let out the reins and Shadow took off. She made a wide but fast turn around the first barrel and headed for the second.

Suddenly Becky caught a flash of something in the dirt just ahead. She pulled Shadow to a sliding stop. "Steady, girl," she soothed.

"What's wrong?" Alison shouted from the sidelines. "Keep going!"

But Becky slid from Shadow's back. The mare had her head down, sniffing at something in the dirt.

"What is it, girl? What's under there?" Becky squatted down and ran her hand through the ground in front of Shadow.

"Ouch!" It was a piece of flexible rubber studded with nails. Becky picked it up and shook off the dirt. There was a murmur in the crowd and then a blur of action. Becky glanced over in time to see Rob holding someone by his shirt collar and hustling him away.

Becky walked Shadow over to the rail and handed the wicked piece of rubber to Sara. "What is this? Could it be what made Sunny and Dark Diamond stumble?"

✳

"How did you know it was Jake Grady?" Becky asked Rob. It was after the races, after Sara and Sunny had won the final, and they were all back at the Twin Rocks trailer.

"Sara and I have had our eyes on him for a while," Rob said, "but we weren't really sure why. After Diane's accident when Sara said Dark Diamond and Sunny stumbled the same way, I got suspicious. Jake Grady rode in both races. It seemed too much of a coincidence that accidents happened when Jake was entered in a race. He's one of those 'win at any price' guys."

"But the junior barrels?" Alison's eyebrows shot up. "That's really sick."

"It was Sunny he was after," Sara said. "He wanted to eliminate us from competition. I'm so lucky that you and Shadow went out first!" She hugged Becky, letting her know she was forgiven.

Alison reached up to stroke Shadow under her shaggy mane. "I'm so glad Becky saw those sharp nails and you're not hurt."

"But it wasn't Jake Grady you grabbed." Becky was still trying to piece it all together. "It was that guy in the green shirt."

Rob grinned at her, his special shy grin that made her heart race. "Jake hired that guy. He volunteers to reset the barrels at these meets. Sometimes he just goes out, moves the barrels around a bit and smooths the dirt around them when they haven't even fallen over. Nobody notices—they just think he's adjusting the barrels. And he's fast setting his booby trap. Even watching, I couldn't actually see him do it."

"Or you would have stopped the race." Becky smiled back.

"Right, but I needed proof. Which, thanks to you and Shadow, we have. Jake Grady won't be hurting any more horses, or people."

"Thanks, little brother." Sara walked over and kissed Rob on his forehead. "We're even now."

Even for what? Becky wondered. She saw the look on Rob's face and knew it wasn't something small. He was beaming at Sara and she was smiling back at him. There was some big secret between those two! Could it have something to do with Rob's illness? she wondered.

"I guess we're even, too, Becky," Alison sighed. "I would have hated falling in the kids' race, in front of all those people."

Everyone laughed, but Alison just looked surprised. "What? What did I say?"

∗

A short e-mail from Meg that night confirmed her plans:

My plane arrives at 9:00 a.m. on the 9th. Can somebody meet me at the airport? I don't go home until the 25th, so I'll have two weeks at Mustang Mountain. I can't wait to see you guys ... and Thomas!

love,
Meg

"The ninth?" Alison stared at the computer screen. "That's your birthday, isn't it?" She turned to Becky. "You'll be fifteen, like me. That's almost sixteen, which is almost eighteen. Soon we'll be able to drive, and vote. We're almost twenty-one!"

Becky grinned. She hadn't realized her birthday was the last day of Stampede. And now Meg was arriving. That was great. If her parents made it down from Mustang Mountain, it would be the perfect fifteenth birthday.

But I'm not like Alison, she thought. I'm not in a rush to grow up. Something tells me there will be heartaches ahead. Like caring too much for Rob, when I can't help him at all!

CHAPTER 22

REUNIONS

"Hurry up!" Becky urged as Alison threw off one set of clothes after another. "It doesn't matter what you wear. We're going to be late to pick up Meg!"

"I want her to see the new me," Alison insisted, wrestling with a red plaid shirt.

"She's not even going to notice you, or me. It's Thomas she wants to see," Becky laughed. "It's great she could save up enough money to get here."

"My riding students," Alison reminded Becky, "took up a collection for her. They've all got tons of money."

"They must really like her." Becky grinned at her cousin. "They're even looking after Patch while she's away."

It was a beautiful July morning and they were headed

to the Calgary airport and then straight to the Stampede grounds, downtown.

Becky was dancing with excitement. It was the last day of the Calgary Stampede *and* her birthday. School was over, and she would soon be going home for the summer. Later today, her parents were arriving in Calgary. Tomorrow they'd drive to the small town near the start of the trail to Mustang Mountain. It was a long ride up to the ranch, but it would be fun with Meg along.

This afternoon, they were all meeting at the Stampede grounds, where they would watch Sara Kelly ride in the finals of the barrel race. Her knee was strong enough for her to ride in the Stampede rodeo, and she'd qualified after a week of difficult races. And Rob would be there, of course.

"I'm ready." Alison did a final spin in front of the mirror. She put on a cowboy hat and tightened her belt. "How do I look?"

"Like a cowgirl," Becky said as they rattled down the stairs. "I hate to admit it, but you're starting to look like the real thing in those clothes."

"I should. I've been here five months." Alison shoved her feet into high-heeled cowboy boots at the front door. "Everybody changes. Two years ago, Meg was lumpy and plain. Now she's tall and gorgeous. And you," Alison looked up and grinned. "You used to be boy-proof. Now you follow Rob Kelly around like a sick puppy."

If you only knew why, Becky thought, but there was truth in Alison's words. Even if she wasn't worried about Rob's health, she would still want to be close to him. Saying good-bye to Rob was the one gray cloud on Becky's birthday.

"I wonder what your dad's going to say about the new you?" Becky teased as they dived into the back seat of the SUV. Alison's father was flying in later today. It wasn't just her longer hair or western clothes that were different. Alison's look of bored elegance was almost gone.

Alison shrugged. "He'll probably have a fit. I don't care, but if he wears a suit to the Stampede, I'm not speaking to him."

Becky laughed. She could just picture her Uncle Roger in a gray pinstripe suit in a sea of blue jeans and cowboy hats.

"Mother says Dad has a big surprise for me." Alison tipped up her chin. "But if they're trying to cook up some scheme to get me back to New York, they can forget it."

Just then her mother opened the car door, cutting short their conversation. "If you two don't mind taking a cab to the Stampede after we find Meg," she told Alison, "I'll stay at the airport and meet your father."

"I'm sure Meg won't mind." Alison smiled. "The sooner she gets to the Stampede grounds, the sooner she'll see Thomas!"

✳

Meg came running through the arrivals area, her knapsack flapping on her shoulder. Becky and Alison enveloped her in a hug.

"Happy birthday, Becky." Meg handed her a small flat parcel wrapped in red paper.

"You remembered!" Becky grinned. "Thanks."

"Of course I remembered. I hope you like it."

"Ahem," Alison cleared her throat loudly, stepped back and twirled around. "What do you think?"

"Alison—wow!" Meg gasped. "I wouldn't have recognized you. You look ... good all duded up."

The three of them caught up on five months of news while they waited for Meg's bags to slide down the luggage ramp. Then they hailed a cab outside the terminal. The taxi dropped them at the gates to Stampede Park, where they joined the crowds streaming through the gate.

"There's Indian Village." Meg's face was suddenly tense. "It's right there, by the river, just where Thomas said it would be."

They could see the tall teepees, clustered in a quiet section of the park near the Elbow River. The rest of the grounds, on the other side of the bridge, was a confusing muddle of flashing lights and country music.

"Drop of Fear," Alison read the sign on a towering midway ride. "That looks like fun."

"There's the grandstand." Becky pointed to the large building that dominated Stampede Park. "That's where all the rodeo events are held."

"The barrel racing finals will go around three o'clock," Alison told Meg. "Wait till you see our friend Sara, and Sunny."

But Meg's eyes were still fixed on the entrance to Indian Village.

"Let's go there first." Becky grinned. "It's still early— we have plenty of time before the finals."

"Thanks," Meg breathed. "I've waited so long to see Thomas."

They walked among the teepees and displays of Aboriginal life on the plains. "There's Wildfire!" Alison pointed. "And Thomas—wow, is he a hunk!"

She would have darted forward, but Becky grabbed her arm. This was Meg's moment. Thomas had changed. He looked older, but still as striking as ever, with his long braid of black hair and his strong, well-defined features.

As he caught sight of Meg and she walked toward him, Becky held her breath. It was as if a powerful magnet were pulling the two of them together. Thomas put down the horse blanket that was draped over his arm. He stretched out both hands to Meg, who walked up to him without a word. They held hands, standing close together.

"Do you think he's going to kiss her?" Alison gasped.

"C'mon," Becky dragged her away. "Let's just go and say hello to Wildfire." She yanked Alison off to greet the big mustang.

"He looks better after a winter of good food." Alison stroked the red stallion's neck. "Look, here are the scars he got fighting with the cougar last summer. But it seems weird to see him with a bridle on and all prettied up. I liked him wild."

Becky fished a horse treat out of her pocket. "So did I, but he wasn't going to survive up there in the wild with cougars and bounty hunters after him." She held the treat out to Wildfire. "Have you been taking good care of Thomas?" she asked him. Wildfire looked at her with a fine, intelligent eye and shook his long mane.

Meg and Thomas came walking up hand in hand. Thomas nodded to Becky. "Happy birthday." He grinned at Alison. "Nice to see you again," he said. "I was getting ready to take Wildfire over to the exhibition barn. Would you like to come along?"

"I would," said Meg.

"You three go ahead," Becky said. "I promised Rob I'd help get Sunny ready for the finals."

Alison pulled a strip of tickets out of her bag. "Here's your rodeo ticket." She tore one off and handed it to Becky. "If we don't meet up with you, we'll see you at the finals."

CHAPTER 23

FINALS

As she ran toward the barns in front of the grandstand, Becky hoped she would be able to find Rob in all the confusion of milling horses and competitors.

When she did, he was riding Sunny.

Becky stood stock-still, staring at him in amazement.

"What's the matter?" he grinned down at her. "You look like you've seen a ghost."

Becky had a mental picture of Rob slamming to the hard ground. She shook it away. "No … I guess I've just never seen you on a horse."

"I guess you haven't." Rob was still grinning, looking back over his shoulder at her as Sunny moved away toward the barn.

"Rob! Watch out!" Sunny was heading for the corner

of a low-hanging eave. Whack! It hit him in the right temple, knocking off his hat.

"That … hurt." Rob clutched his head.

Becky saw with horror that there was blood on his fingers. For a second, the world spun. Then Becky heard herself screaming, "Help, somebody, help! He'll bleed to death. He's bleeding, oh—"

She felt Rob's hand clamped over her mouth. He had jumped off Sunny and was holding a handkerchief to his head with his other hand.

"Will you stop that!" He took his hand away from her mouth and grabbed for Sunny's loose reins. "What is the matter with you, Becky Sandersen? It's just a scratch."

"But you can't get scratched," Becky managed to splutter. "You could bleed to death."

"What are you babbling about?" Rob was blotting his forehead with the handkerchief. "Head wounds always bleed, but it's not fatal."

"But your condition, your thrombocytopenia!"

"My thrombo—what? What in blazes are you talking about?"

"Your c-condition," stammered Becky, "where you bruise easily and could hemorrhage."

"If I had a condition like that, don't you think I'd know about it?" Rob dabbed at his forehead again. There was a lot of blood but it wasn't gushing. In fact, it already seemed to be slowing down.

"You're not … sick?" Becky gasped.

"Of course not. Whatever gave you that crazy idea?" Rob was almost shouting.

"You're always going to the doctor, and you don't ride Sunny, at least you didn't, and you wear a medic-alert thing around your neck." The words burst out of Becky's lips.

"Oh, for Pete's sake," Rob groaned. "I go to the doctor for checkups because I had mono last year and I'm still a bit anemic. This is a St. Christopher's medal my mom gave me." He yanked the necklace out to show her.

"That's all? I'm so glad!" Becky could feel a huge bubble of happiness inside. This was the best birthday she could ever have. Rob didn't have a deadly disease. He was fine. She told him about Alison's suspicions and Meg's Web research.

"So that's how it started." Rob shook his head. "With you wondering why I didn't ride Sunny for Sara, and Alison egging you on."

"I'm sorry—it was stupid not to just ask you," Becky apologized.

"That's all right. It was my fault, too, for being so stubborn about riding Sara's horse." Rob gave a wry grin. "The trouble with these bossy, takeover people like my sister and your cousin is that they keep getting you in situations where you look bad."

Becky felt giddy. "You're right. Half the dumb things I do these days are because Alison's pushed me into a corner."

"And it can last for years," Rob went on. "When I was

fourteen, Sara and I fought over a horse we both wanted —something like you and Alison wanting Shadow. And then I injured that horse—like you riding Shadow into a fence. Sara accused me of ruining him for barrel racing. So I swore I'd never ride another horse of hers again."

"Now I understand." Becky was still smiling. "When you caught Jake Grady, and Sara said, 'Now we're even,' she was talking about that old fight. And that's why you're riding Sunny now?"

"That's right." Rob gave a sudden start. "Hey! Speaking of Sara's horses, I'd better get Sunny back to her—she wanted to warm him up herself."

"You'd better let me help clean you up first." Becky pointed to his head. "You look like you've been in an accident."

"Tell me," Rob said as she gently sponged the blood off his face in the tack room, "do you still like me now that you know I'm not dying of a horrible disease?"

"What made you think I liked you?" Becky grinned at him.

✳

Leaving Rob to find Sara, Becky climbed to her seat high in the third level of the grandstand. The sky over Calgary was a dome of pure blue. The crowd was a sea of cowboy hats. Everybody wore them: ranchers, rodeo people, tourists, even little kids.

Becky saw her mother waving from their seats. She had managed to get seats for all of them together.

Becky scrambled over people's knees and fell into her mom's arms laughing, she was so glad to finally see her parents.

"I'm sorry it took us so long to get away from Mustang Mountain," her dad hollered into her ear. "We've been so darned shorthanded at the ranch this spring."

"It's all right." Becky hugged him hard. "You're here now, and I'm going home."

Alison was sitting between her parents. Becky choked back a giggle. Roger Chant *was* wearing a gray suit with a white cowboy hat that looked brand new. It perched on his head as if it never meant to settle down and get comfortable.

"Did you find Rob?" Meg's eyes were full of concern as Becky slid in beside her.

Becky knew she was feeling sympathetic about Rob's condition, and she wished she could grab her friend and pour out her good news. But she didn't want to talk about it in front of everybody, so she just said "I found him, he's fine."

"The barrel racing finals will be exciting." Laurie Sandersen's eyes sparkled. "Sara Kelly's up against some stiff competition. That Tammy Talon from Montana has won the fifty-thousand-dollar prize twice in the last three years."

"Sara's been working hard," Becky said. "She's young, but she's really good."

"And Sunny's an amazing horse. I rode him." Alison was leaning forward, clutching her knees.

Her parents glanced at each other over her head. Uncle Roger looked totally confused at the change in his daughter, Becky thought. Even Aunt Marion looked different. For the first time, she and Becky's mother actually looked like sisters. They were both wearing sleeveless T-shirts and blue jeans. Alison was right. Everybody changed.

Becky could see Rob down in the competitors' area, talking to Sara up on Sunny. They shook hands. Becky felt a lump in her throat. It was a good thing they had made up, even though Sara would probably go right on being the bossy big sister. Well, maybe some people never changed.

Five riders rode before Sara. The time to beat was Tammy Talon's.

The crowd roared as Sunny and Sara came flying through the gate. They were the hometown favorites. The second barrel rocked as Sara risked riding too close to cut a fraction of a second off her time. Thousands of people gasped.

But the second barrel didn't fall. There was a roar of relief.

Sara tore for the finish line, bent low on the golden horse.

Silence, while thousands waited for the official time announcement. Cheers when she beat Tammy's time by 0.05 of a second. Enough to beat Tammy, but would it hold for the last four riders? Only one would go home with fifty thousand dollars in her pocket.

The first rider after Sara was having a good ride until she knocked over the third barrel.

The next barrel racer, a girl from Arizona, knocked over the first. The next had trouble getting off to a good start. Her time was much slower than Sara's.

They were down to the last rider.

Becky couldn't stand the suspense. She held her breath and clutched Meg's arm while the woman on the chestnut stallion zoomed around the barrels with no faults.

Now there was absolute silence. They could see the time on the clock, but everyone was waiting for the official announcement—it was so close to Sara's.

"Time of the last ride was 14.08 seconds."

Sara had won!

Wild cheering burst out from every throat. Sara rode back into the ring and made a slow loping circle on Sunny, waving her hat. People stood and whistled and stomped. Becky thumped Meg's back. "She did it! She did it!"

"I rode that horse." They could hear Alison's shrill cry above the cheering. "And I'm going to be here someday, on Shadow."

CHAPTER 24

STAMPEDE NIGHT

After Sara had gone up on stage to accept her check and trophy, Becky, Alison and Meg raced down to the barn, where she was cooling out Sunny. Rob was fending off the press so that his sister could have a few minutes to recover, but he let the three girls through with a smile. "She'll want to see you."

Sara was transformed. The look of strain and worry that she always wore was gone, and she was radiant in triumph. She wanted to talk about the race.

"It was all Sunny." She leaned over his golden mane. "It was really all Sunny's doing. He had a great day and that made up for the weakness in my knee. I just had to let him go. We got lucky with that second barrel!" She sat up straight and grinned. "I cut it too close, but luck held it up."

Sara reached down and grabbed Alison's shoulder. "Thanks for being my inspiration," she said. "When I saw you riding Sunny, I realized how great he was. I just had to get strong enough to ride him."

Becky could see that the powerful, never-give-up quality in Sara was the same thing that made her bossy. Alison had it, too, that fierce focus that shut everyone else out. She'd probably be a champion like Sara someday.

Sara turned to Becky. "And you." She shook her head. "I don't know what went on behind the scenes, but something tells me you're the one I really have to thank."

She glanced over to where Rob was still holding back a swarm of photographers. "At the very least, you brought my brother out of the sad place he's been since Mom and Dad died." Sara slipped from Sunny's back and threw her arms around Becky. "Rob's all full of plans and schemes—just like the old days. He even says he'd like to visit your wilderness ranch."

Becky nodded. "It would be great if he could. Meg and her friend Thomas and I are all going together, and I know Rob wants to see my dad's mountain horse breeding program."

"I guess it's okay," Sara laughed. "Just don't forget, I need him back—he's going to be my right-hand man on the barrel racing circuit for the rest of the summer."

We'll see about that, Becky thought. One of the things about these bossy, self-centered people is that they don't see what's right under their noses. Rob doesn't want to be anybody's right-hand man. He wants to be his own man! She was eager to get her dad and Rob together. She had a scheme of her own in mind.

"Can we borrow Rob for an hour or so right now?" she asked. She wanted Meg to get to know Rob.

"I guess so." Sara looked unsure for a second and then laughed. "I can face those cameras now. I think Sunny and I are going to have to get used to it."

*

They prowled the midway, Becky and Rob, Alison and Meg. There were lots of games where you could try to win a stuffed animal. There was cotton candy and delicious hot little doughnuts called Tom Thumbs. The air was filled with wonderful smells and music.

"I wish I wasn't having dinner with my parents." Alison was stuffing herself with an enormous steak sandwich. "This is what I really like to eat, and I hate to miss the chuckwagon races."

"Your dad still hasn't told you his big surprise. Don't you want to find out?" asked Meg.

"I suppose so," sighed Alison. "But something tells me I'm not going to like it."

"Meg and I are meeting my parents at the chuckwagon races later," Becky told Rob. "Can you come?"

"I never miss the chucks," Rob promised. "But I should get back to Sara and Sunny. I'll see you there." He strolled away with his long-legged stride.

Meg watched him go. "What did you mean when you said Rob was fine?" she asked Becky. "What about his thrombo ...?"

Becky coughed to interrupt. "Uh, Alison doesn't know about Rob's condition."

"What condition? What are you two talking about?" Alison was suddenly all ears.

"We thought Rob had—some kind of—awful disease," Becky stammered. "You know, because you called him Sickly Rob, and everything."

"You took that seriously?" Alison laughed. "I was just teasing. There's nothing wrong with Rob that a few barbecued beef sandwiches wouldn't fix." She waved her sandwich in the air.

"It's not a joke," Meg was indignant. "He could die from this disease."

"But he doesn't have it," Becky hurried to explain. "I just found out. He goes to the doctor because he was anemic last year, and the bruises on his arms are from Chompster bites, and he didn't ride Sunny because of an old fight with Sara!" She stopped, breathless. "I just ... got the idea he was sick and Meg found the symptoms of this thrombo-thing on the Web."

"Rob is really all right?" Meg was staring at her with wide blue eyes.

Becky nodded. "He's fine. Perfect, in fact." She could feel herself blushing.

"Wow, what a relief." Meg shook back her ponytail. "I'll never diagnose from the Internet again."

"So that's what all the secret e-mails were about?" Alison said. "You two are idiots!"

*

They all met that night at the top of the grandstand. Thomas came, too—he had friends who competed in the chuckwagon races every year.

Meg looked blissful. The prospect of going to Mustang Mountain Ranch for a couple of weeks and seeing Thomas there was more than she had dared to hope for.

The sun was setting, throwing a rosy glow over the midway and the office towers of downtown Calgary. On the other side of the Stampede grounds, the Elbow River bluff stood against the sky. It was a beautiful summer night, and the races were about to start. Horses and chuckwagons milled around below them.

This was the perfect time to introduce Rob to her dad and set her plan in motion, Becky thought.

"Dad, this is Rob Kelly. He's an amazing horseman—he can train horses and he grew up on a breeding ranch, so he knows his stuff."

"Wait a second." Rob was blushing to the tips of his ears. "Pleased to meet you, Mr. Sandersen. Becky sounds like she's trying to get me a job."

"That's exactly right." Becky grinned. "Dad's short-handed right now—"

"I sure am," Dan Sandersen broke in. "I don't suppose you would be interested in a job for the summer up at our ranch? It's pretty isolated—in a wildlife preserve, so there's no vehicles allowed—not much like life down here." He gestured to the packed stands and the city beyond.

Rob looked from Dan to Becky. A slow smile lit up his face. "She's told me all about Mustang Mountain. It sounds great." He nodded, holding out his hand. "Yes, sir, I definitely would be interested in a job at your ranch."

"Then we'll talk after the races." Dan shook the young man's hand.

Becky and her mom, Laurie, shared a grin. "I think this will work out fine," said Laurie. "We sure can use the help."

"There's Alison!" Meg cried, pointing to the aisle, where Alison was squirming her way past many pairs of feet.

"I made it! We had an early dinner and I made Mother and Dad drive me back so I could tell you the news!" Alison's face was alive with excitement. She squeezed into Meg's seat, which was really only big enough for one. "Guess what my father's surprise was?"

They all stared at her, waiting.

"Would you believe, a whole month in Paris, just Dad and me! He's got reservations in one of the best hotels, and we'll do trips to Versailles and other places—I've always wanted to go to France, the shopping's supposed to be fabulous—"

"What about barrel racing, and Shadow?" Becky

stopped her in mid-flow. "Are you moving back to New York?"

"Are Marion and Roger getting back together?" Becky's mother asked.

"Who knows? They're not at that stage, yet. Dad and I are going to have this trip, first," Alison said breezily. "I can get back to barrel racing after. And Rob can look after Shadow while I'm gone."

It was getting hard to talk with the roar of the crowd erupting as the first chuckwagon heat started. "Rob's coming to Mustang Mountain!" Becky shouted. "He's going to work there for the summer."

"Can you take Shadow up there with you?" Alison shouted back. "Sara's going to be too busy to take care of her."

Shadow at Mustang Mountain! Becky sat back in her seat and let the roar of the crowd fade into the background as she pictured how wonderful it would be. "Sure we can!" she hollered at last. "I hope you have a great time in Paris. Good for your dad."

"Can you believe he bought a cowboy hat? He looks silly, but he's trying." Alison gave a happy shrug.

The chuckwagons had finished their turns around the barrels. They streamed out along the racetrack with their outriders behind. It was a thrilling scene and people were on their feet, screaming encouragement to their favorite teams. Becky sat, feeling Rob close beside her, happy with the thought of the glorious summer ahead. This was definitely the best birthday of her life.

ABOUT THE AUTHOR

As a kid, Sharon Siamon was horse crazy. How crazy? She never walked—she galloped everywhere on an imaginary horse. At school, she organized a whole gang of riders, who headed for the ranch in the corner of the school yard every recess and lunch hour to play horses. At home she lured the huge workhorses on her neighbor's farm over to the fence with apples, then clambered on their backs and rode like the wind until they scraped her off under a low-hanging hawthorn tree. She grew up, still wishing for a horse and taking every chance she got to get near horses, read about horses and ride them. She's been writing horse books ever since for kids who love to dream about having a horse of their own.

Sharon is the author of many books, including eight Sleepover Series titles and a number of Stage School Series titles under the pseudonym Geena Dare. The Mustang Mountain series has already been translated into German, Finnish, Norwegian and Swedish.

COLLECT ALL THE MUSTANG MOUNTAIN BOOKS!

Mustang Mountain #1: Sky Horse (1-55285-456-6)

Meg, her friend Alison and Alison's cousin Becky must make a journey on horseback to the Mustang Mountain Ranch in the Rocky Mountains. A sudden storm, an icy road—an adventure begins that will take the three girls off the beaten track to where cougars, grizzlies and wild mustangs roam free.

Mustang Mountain #2: Fire Horse (1-55285-457-4)

Meg, Alison and Becky search the wilderness for two horses that have disappeared from the ranch. Suddenly, a bolt of lightning sets the forest ablaze and they must use all their courage and ingenuity to save themselves and their horses.

Mustang Mountain #3: Night Horse (1-55285-363-2)

Meg, Alison and Becky return to Mustang Mountain Ranch for the summer, where a beautiful mare named Windy is about to give birth to her first foal. It isn't long before a chance meeting with a young rancher lets Meg in on an explosive secret: a bounty hunter has been hired to kill the wild horses that roam the hills. But when Windy escapes from the ranch, it falls upon the girls to protect the mare and the wild stallion, Wildfire.

Mustang Mountain #4: Wild Horse (1-55285-413-2)

Alison's father has sold her prized horse, Duchess. Becky is homesick for her family and Mustang Mountain. Meg just wants a horse of her own. Then the three girls get the chance to travel to Wyoming and get to know some real wild horses. Alison's fury over losing Duchess recedes a little when she finds a horse that needs her, but nothing comes easy on this trip.